EXPOSED!

In the Oval Room of the White House, the President watched the press conference live on television. When the reporter mentioned the word "Folcroft," the President's face became ashen.

How did it happen? Miami Beach had been their breakthrough. For over two years, CURE had been drawing in raw reports from FBI agents, CIA agents, agricultural, postal, IRS and SEC investigators, and feeding them into a computer, programmed to collate and interpret them, and then sending its conclusions on to Kansas City in code. No one should have known, but he realized what had happened. Smith had been careless.

THE DESTROYER SERIES:

- #1 CREATED, THE DESTROYER
- #2 DEATH CHECK
- #3 CHINESE PUZZLE
- #4 MAFIA FIX
- #5 DR. QUAKE
- #6 DEATH THERAPY
- #7 UNION BUST
- #8 SUMMIT CHASE
- #9 MURDER'S SHIELD
- #10 TERROR SQUAD
- #11 KILL OR CURE
- #12 SLAVE SAFARI
- #13 ACID ROCK
- #14 JUDGMENT DAY
- #15 MURDER WARD
- #16 OIL SLICK
- #17 LAST WAR DANCE
- #18 FUNNY MONEY
- #19 HOLY TERROR
- #20 ASSASSIN'S PLAY-OFF
- #21 DEADLY SEEDS
- #22 BRAIN DRAIN
- #23 CHILD'S PLAY
- #24 KING'S CURSE
- #25 SWEET DREAMS
- #26 IN ENEMY HANDS
- #27 THE LAST TEMPLE
- #28 SHIP OF DEATH
- #29 THE FINAL DEATH
- #30 MUGGER BLOOD
- #31 THE HEAD MEN
- #32 KILLER CHROMOSOMES
- #33 VOODOO DIE
- #34 CHAINED REACTION
- #35 LAST CALL
- #36 POWER PLAY
- #37 BOTTOM LINE
- #38 BAY CITY BLAST
- #39 MISSING LINK
- #40 DANGEROUS GAMES
- #41 FIRING LINE
- #42 TIMBER LINE
- #43 MIDNIGHT MAN
- #44 BALANCE OF POWER
- #45 SPOILS OF WAR
- #46 NEXT OF KIN
- #47 DYING SPACE

ATTENTION: SCHOOLS AND CORPORATIONS

PINNACLE Books are available at quantity discounts with bulk purchases for educational, business or special promotional use. For further details, please write to: SPECIAL SALES MANAGER, Pinnacle Books, Inc., 1430 Broadway, New York, NY 10018

WRITE FOR OUR FREE CATALOG

If there is a Pinnacle Book you want—and you cannot find it locally—it is available from us simply by sending the title and price plus 75¢ to cover mailing and handling costs to:

    Pinnacle Books, Inc.
    Reader Service Department
    1430 Broadway
    New York, NY 10018

Please allow 6 weeks for delivery.

—— Check here if you want to receive our catalog regularly.

THE DESTROYER #11
KILL OR CURE

by
Warren Murphy

PINNACLE BOOKS • **NEW YORK**

This is a work of fiction. All the characters and events portrayed in this book are fictional, and any resemblance to real people or incidents is purely coincidental.

THE DESTROYER: KILL OR CURE

Copyright © 1973 by Richard Sapir and Warren Murphy

All rights reserved, including the right to reproduce this book or portions thereof in any form.

An original Pinnacle Books edition, published for the first time anywhere.

ISBN: 0-523-41856-6

First printing, August 1973
Second printing, March 1974
Third printing, July 1974
Fourth printing, October 1975
Fifth printing, February 1977
Sixth printing, April 1978
Seventh printing, April 1979
Eighth printing, September 1980
Ninth printing, December 1981

Printed in the United States of America

PINNACLE BOOKS, INC.
1430 Broadway
New York, New York 10018

With the exception of the House of Sinanju, any resemblance between characters and events and any persons living or dead is purely coincidental.

FOR PAUL:
        SURSUM CORDA

AND FOR:
    COLLEEN, REGGIE, ALLISON,
    MOKIE, GUS &
    THE GIRL FROM SASKATCHEWAN.

CHAPTER ONE

James Bullingsworth had entertained few original thoughts in his life, but his last one was good enough to get him an ice pick in his brain, send a multitude of government agents fleeing to obscure outposts, and leave the president of the United States gasping:

"Why do these things always have to happen to me?"

This particular doozy of an idea came to James Bullingsworth one morning in late spring while doing volunteer work for the Greater Florida Betterment League where he had been volunteering nine to five, Monday through Friday, for the last two years. That Bullingsworth tended not to probe too deeply into the reasons of things was why he got the job, and before he started thinking new things, he should have remembered how he had volunteered.

The volunteer ceremony had been brief. The president of the bank where Bullingsworth worked had called him into his office.

"Bullingsworth, what do you think of improving the government of the greater Miami area?" the president had asked.

Bullingsworth had thought improvement was a good idea.

"Bullingsworth, how would you like to volunteer your time and effort to the Greater Florida Betterment League?"

Bullingsworth would like to do that, but it might interfere with his career at the bank.

"Bullingsworth, *that is* your career at the bank."

So James Bullingsworth, who was known to mind his

own business, went to work for the League while he drew his paychecks from the bank. He should have remembered the strangeness of his appointment that spring morning when he noticed a computer printout was incomplete.

He said to his secretary, a young Cuban woman with very high breasts: "Miss Carbonal, this computer printout is incomplete. There are great gaps in it. It's just a bunch of random letters. We can't forward it in this condition."

Miss Carbonal picked up the greenish printout and stared at it. Bullingsworth stared at her left breast. She was wearing the see-through bra again.

"We always send it out like this," said Miss Carbonal.

"What?" said Bullingsworth.

"We been sending out printouts like this for two years now. When we mail to the Kansas City office, it's always like this. I speak to the other girls at other Betterment League offices all around the country and they say the same. At Kansas City, they must be some crazy people, yes?"

"Let me see that breast," said Bullingsworth, with authority.

"Wha?" said Miss Carbonal.

"The printout," said Bullingsworth, covering up his slip quickly. "Let me see it." He busied himself in the random letters with the big gaps. "Hmmmmm," said James Bullingsworth, former assistant vice-president of one of the larger banks in the greater Miami area. The idea was born.

"Miss Carbonal, I want you to get me all the printouts shipped from our office to Kansas City."

"What you want that for?"

"Miss Carbonal, I gave you an instruction."

"You be in plenty trouble, asking questions. You want to look at those printouts, you go yourself."

"Are you refusing a direct order, Miss Carbonal?"

"You betcha, Mr. Bullingsworth."

"That's all I wanted to hear," said Bullingsworth menacingly. "You may leave."

Miss Carbonal fluffed out undisturbed. A half-hour later as Bullingsworth left for lunch, she called to him:

"Mr. Bullingsworth, don't go rocking the boat. You got good money. I got good money. We don't ask questions. What do you want?"

Bullingsworth approached her desk with great gravity.

"Miss Carbonal," he said. "There are ways to do things. Proper, businesslike, thorough ways to do things. There are American ways to do things and that means knowing what you're doing and not just dumbly—animal-like—sending off garbled printouts for two years. It means, Miss Carbonal, understanding what you are doing."

"You're a nice man, Mr. Bullingsworth. Take my word for it. Don't go rocking the boat. Okay?"

"No," said Bullingsworth.

"You can't get those other printouts anyway. Henrietta Alvarez is the girl who does them. She feeds them into the computer, checks the printout to make sure it's accurate and then destroys it. That's what she was told to do. And she was told to report anyone asking questions about the printouts."

"You don't understand Yankee pluck, Miss Carbonal."

James Bullingsworth exercised Yankee pluck that night after all the other League employees had left the office. He broke into the locked desk of Henrietta Alvarez and, as he had suspected, found inside a foot-high compression of light-green printouts.

Amused at his secretary's apprehension, Bullingsworth took the thick pile of printouts into his office for inspection. His confidence soared as he read the first line of each printout.

They obviously were in code and he, James Bullingsworth, would break that code for his amusement. He needed a diversion, in a job that occupied only two hours of each working day. Incredible that anyone could think such a thing could escape his notice for long, he thought. Were they fools at the National Betterment League's headquarters in Kansas City?

The code proved to be quite simple, almost like a crossword puzzle. Putting a week's printouts together at once, the gaps on the lines were filled. The only question was which order the letters must be read in.

"Tragf pu," scribbled Bullingsworth, and with that he rearranged the sheets again. "Fargt up," and he rearranged them again.

"Graft up," wrote Bullingsworth. Without rearranging the computer printouts again, he began to copy down the contents of the sheets. He worked all night long. When he was finished, he scrambled the sheets and read his handiwork.

"Jeeezus H. Christ," he whistled. He looked through the glass door connecting his office with outside, saw Miss Carbonal arriving for work, and waved her to come inside.

"Carmen, Carmen. Look at this. Look at what I figured out."

Carmen Carbonal stuck her fingers in her ears and rushed from the office. "Don't tell me nothing," she yelled.

He followed her to her desk. "Hey, don't be afraid," he said.

"You *muy stupido*," she said. "You big, stupid man. Burn that stuff. Burn that stuff."

"Aren't you interested in what we're really doing?"

"No," she cried, sobbing. "I don't want to know. And you shouldn't want to know either. You so dumb. Dumb."

"Oh, Carmen," said Bullingsworth, placing a comforting arm around her heaving shoulder. "I'm sorry. If it'll make you feel better, I'll burn everything."

"Too late," she said. "Too late."

"It's not too late," he said. "I'll burn it now."

"Too late."

With great fanfare, Bullingsworth brought all the copies of the printouts to the private bathroom in his office and burned them, creating lung-choking smoke.

"Now are you happy?" he asked Miss Carbonal.

"Too late," she said, still weeping.

"I burned everything," he smiled.

But Bullingsworth had not burned everything. He had saved his notes, which, among other things, told him why his bank was willing to pay him a salary for volunteer work with the Greater Florida Betterment League. It also told him why so many Florida officials had suddenly been so successfully indicted for kickbacks and extortion. It even gave him a hint as to how the upcoming local elections would come out, and why.

Bullingsworth suddenly felt very proud of his country, secure knowing that America was doing more to fight the disintegration of the nation than met the eye. Much more.

Only one thing in the notes bothered him. That was the section on proposed pay raises for approval by "Folcroft," whatever or whoever "Folcroft" was.

Everyone at his level in the League was getting a 14 percent raise and his was a non-inflationary 2.5 percent. He decided he wasn't going to let it bother him, because he shouldn't have been aware of the injustice anyway. He would put it out of his mind. And if had had done this thing as he had planned, he would have lived to collect his non-inflationary 2.5 percent pay raise.

But his resolve disappeared later that day when he met the President of the Greater Miami Trust and Investment Company and wondered why he had received only a 2.5 per cent raise. The president, who considered himself an expert in industrial and human relations, told Bullingsworth he was sorry but no one on loan to the Betterment League was getting more than 2.5 percent.

"Are you sure?" said Bullingsworth.

"I give you my word as a banker. Have I ever lied to you?"

The first thing James Bullingsworth did was have a drink. A martini. Double. Then he had another martini. And another after that. And when he arrived home, he told his wife that if she mentioned he had been drinking, he would punch her heart out, noted that she had been right all along about how the bank was using him, put on a fresh jacket—carefully transferring his notebook to the inside pocket—and flailed out of the house yelling how he was "going to show those sons of bitches who James Bullingsworth was."

At first he played with the idea of exposing the Betterment League in the *Miami Dispatch*. But that could get him fired. Then he thought of confronting the president of the bank. That would get him the increased money, but somewhere along the road the bank president would make him suffer.

The proper course of action came to him when he switched to bourbon. Bourbon focused the mind, elevated it to awarenesses of human relationships not understood in mere gin and vermouth.

Bourbon told him that it was every man for himself. It was the law of the jungle. And he, James Bullingsworth, had been a fool to think he lived in a civilized society. A fool. Did the bartender know that?

"We're cutting you off, Mister," said the bartender.

"Then you're the fool," Bullingsworth said. "Beware the king of the jungle," he said, and remembering a Miami Beach official who once spoke at a church picnic and said he was glad to see young men like James Bullingsworth get involved in civic affairs, he phoned that official.

"Why don't we talk this over in the morning, huh, fella?" said the official.

"Because, baby, you may not be around in the morning. They're going to indict your ass next. Parking meter receipts."

"Maybe we'd better not talk about this on the phone. Where can we meet?"

"I want a million dollars for what I have. A cool million, buddy, because this is the law of the jungle."

"Do you know the Mall in Miami Beach, the end of the Mall?"

"Do I know the Mall? Do you know what you people are planning for construction on Key Biscayne? Do I know the Mall?"

"Look, fella, at the end of the Mall, on the beach near the Ritz Hotel. Can you get there in an hour?"

"I can get there in fifteen minutes."

"No, don't get in any accidents. I think you've got something very valuable."

"A million dollars valuable," said Bullingsworth, drunkenly slurring the words. "A million dollars."

He hung up and, while passing the bar, informed the bartender that he just might come back, buy the bar and fire his Irish ass the hell out of there. He waved the notebook with the scribbles in front of the bartender's face.

"It's all here, sweetheart. Gonna fire your Irish ass the hell out of here. Gonna be the biggest political cat in the political jungle. You'll think another think before you cut off James Bullingsworth. Where's the door?"

"You're leaning on it," said the bartender.

"Right," said Bullingsworth and sailed out into the muggy Miami night. The air had a bit of a sobering effect on him and by the time he reached the beach he was only drunk. He kicked the sand and breathed the fresh salt-air. Maybe he had been a bit precipitous? He looked at his watch. He could use another drink. He could really use another drink. Maybe if he went to the president of the bank, explained what he did, maybe everything could be worked out.

He heard the strains of Bette Midler from an open hotel room window. He heard a small power-boat approaching. The beach was supposed to be lit at this hour. All the other sections were indeed well-lighted, but this section was dark. The Atlantic was black out there, with a lone ship blinking like an island afloat.

Then came a whisper.

"Bullingsworth. Bullingsworth. Is that you?"

"Yeah. Is that you?" said Bullingsworth.

"Yes."

"Where are you?"

"Never mind. Did you bring the information?"

"Yes, I have it."

"You tell anyone else?"

Sobering up all too quickly, Bullingsworth thought about an answer. If he told them someone else knew about it, then they might think he was blackmailing them. Then again, that was what he was doing.

"Look, never mind," said Bullingsworth. "We'll talk about this some other day. I'm not going to tell anyone else. Let's meet tomorrow."

"What do you have?"

"Nothing. I didn't bring it."

"What's that notebook?"

"Oh, this. Jeez. Just to take notes. I always carry one."

"Let me see it."

"No," said Bullingsworth.

"You don't want me to take it, do you?"

"Just notes. Notes I have."

"Bring it here."

"They're nothing, really. I mean, nothing. Look, my friends are going to pick me up here any minute. I'll be seeing you. Tomorrow is fine," said Bullingsworth. "I'm really sorry to have bothered an important man like you tonight anyway."

"Bring the notebook over here, James," came the voice, soft and ominous and tinged, Bullingsworth realized for the first time, with a touch of Europe. "You'll be sorry if I have to go over there and get it."

The voice was so threatening that Bullingsworth, like a little boy, meekly entered the darkness.

"Just notes," he said.

"Tell me about them."

Bullingsworth smelled the lilac cologne very heavy. The man was shorter than he, by about an inch, but broader, and there was something in his tone—something in the way he spoke—that was commanding. He was, of course, not the politician that Bullingsworth had expected to meet.

"They're just notes," Bullingsworth said. "From a computer printout in the Betterment League."

"Who else knows you made the notes?"

"No one," said Bullingsworth, knowing he was saving his secretary's life, just as he knew his own life would be soon over. It was as if he were a spectator to the event. He knew what would happen, there was nothing he could do, and now he was watching himself about to be killed. It didn't seem horrible at all. There was something beyond horror, like the acceptance of it.

"Not even your secretary, Miss Carbonal?"

"Miss Carbonal is a hear-no-evil, see-no-evil, nine-to-five, pick-up-your-check-and-go-home type. You know, Cuban."

"Yes, I know. These printouts. What do they say?"

"They show that the National Betterment League is a fake. A secret government organization that's investigating and infiltrating local governments in cities all across the country."

"And what about Miami Beach?"

"The Greater Florida Betterment League is a cover,

too. It's been digging into political crime in Miami Beach. Shakedowns, gambling, extortion. It's been setting up a case against all the city officials, getting evidence ready for indictments."

"I see. Anything else?"

"No. No. That's about it."

"Would you like to work for us?"

"Sure," said Bullingsworth, as sober as he had ever drawn a sober breath.

"Would you like your money now?"

"Now. Anytime."

"I see. Look at that boat behind you. Out there, in the Atlantic. Look."

Bullingsworth saw the boat, placid and blinking in the vast darkness.

"I don't believe you," said the man with the heavy lilac cologne and the foreign accent, and then Bullingsworth felt a sharp sting in his right ear, and saw nothing else. But, in the vast nothing that is death is often infinite wisdom, and in his last thought he knew that his killer would face an awesome force that would grind him and his cohorts into waste material, a force that was at the very center of the universe. Of course, all of this meant very little to James Bullingsworth, former assistant vice-president of the Greater Miami Trust and Investment Company. He was dead.

In the course of normal, morning, beach-cleaning operations, Bullingsworth's body was discovered with what appeared to be a wooden tool handle in his ear.

"Oh, no," said the sweeper and decided immediately he would not act like some hysterical woman. He would walk calmly to the nearest telephone and call the police, giving them exact details and other useful information.

This resolve to discipline lasted three steps on the sandy beach, whereupon it was discarded for an alternate course of action.

"Help. Arggghh. Dead. Help. Body. Help. Someone. Police. Help."

The sweeper might have stayed rooted, screaming until he was hoarse, but an elderly vacationer spotted him and the body from her hotel window and phoned the police.

"Better bring an ambulance too," she said. "There's a hysterical man down there."

The police brought more than an ambulance. They brought photographers and reporters and television crews. For something had happened during the night to make the death of this man a very important matter, important enough to call a press conference where James Bullingsworth's doozy of an idea—his belief in a federal government plot to infiltrate local governments and jail key officials—got a public airing.

Waving the Bullingsworth notes before the heavy lights of TV camera crews, who were paid overtime for the pre-dawn work, a local politician of minor rank talked ominously of the "most treacherous act of government interference in the history of our nation."

CHAPTER TWO

His name was Remo and he intended to interfere with local government very much. He intended to make it do its job.

He rested his toes in the brick crevices, and with his charcoal-blackened hands pressed flat against the rough brick, kept his balance outside the window. He could smell the heavy fumes of Boston. He could feel the vibrations of the traffic down below in the dampish night street through the building wall, and he wished he were in some place warm and sunny, like Miami Beach. But his assignment was Boston. First things first.

A passerby, fourteen stories below in front of the hotel, would never see this figure pressed into the wall, for he wore black shoes, black pants and black shirt, and his face and hands were blackened with a charcoal paste given him by the man who had taught him that the side of a building could be a ladder if the mind knew how to use it as one.

Voices came from the open window near his right kneecap. The window should not have been open, but then the two detectives and plainclothesmen hadn't done their job very well from the beginning.

"You're sure I'm okay here, fellas?" asked a man in a rough, rock voice.

That was Vincent Tomalino, Remo knew.

"Sure. You got us with you all the time," said another man. Must be one of the cops, Remo thought.

"Okay," said Tomalino, but his voice lacked conviction.

"Wanna play some cards?" asked one of the cops.

"No," said Tomalino. "You sure that window should be open?"

"Sure, sure. Fresh air."

"We can use the air conditioner."

"Lookit, you guinea stool pigeon, don't tell us our jobs." It struck Remo as amusing that those officers with the heaviest service to the Mafia were always the freest to use terms like "guinea," "wop," and "dago."

Upstairs probably had some psychological report on that. They had reports on everything it seemed, from parking-meter graft in Miami Beach to ex-Mafiosi who were going to be rubbed out because they planned to talk.

Tomalino was going to talk.

On this, there were several opinions. The district attorney promised the papers Tomalino would probably spill, but the three policemen had promised the local *capo mafioso* that he wouldn't. These opinions were really just opinions because it had been decided in an office in Folcroft Sanitarium in Rye, New York, that Vincent "The Blast" Tomalino not only would talk, but he would tell everything he knew with a pure heart.

"I want to check the window," said Tomalino.

"Stay where you are," said one of the cops. "You two keep him on the bed. I'm going to check the roof."

Remo looked up to the roof. Surprise, surprise—here it came. A rope swooped out in an arch and slapped back against the side of the hotel. It paused there a moment, a head peered over and the rope descended, right past Remo's knee. He heard the hotel room door open and close, and assumed the officer was going up to the roof to get his payoff immediately after the job was done.

A large body grunted its way over the ledge and using hands and feet like clumsy logs lowered itself down the rope. Remo could smell the man's meat-eating breath from five feet away. A carbine which could be handled with one hand was strapped to the man's back. And there was something metallic around his waist. What was it? Remo peered more closely. The man had attached a pulley to his waist so he wouldn't fall.

Remo couldn't get the idea of meat out of his mind. He hadn't had a steak for two years. Oh, for a juicy-fat crisp steak, or rich thick hamburger, or a slice of quivering roast beef oozing its juices from a delicious red center. Even a hot dog would be great. Or a slice of bacon, a magnificent slice of bacon.

The meat-eater's right foot touched the top of the window and still he did not see Remo. He reached for the carbine on his back and since he seemed to be having trouble, Remo helped him.

"It's stuck," said Remo, reaching up, but not for the carbine.

He got the pulley with his right hand, snapping it off, and since there was no need for loud unpleasantness, he took out the meat-eater's throat with a thumb on the way down.

Like a water-filled balloon from a conventioneer's window, the meat-eater plummeted—arms and legs flailing noiselessly—to the pavement below. Concrete and killer were joined with a muffled splat.

Remo climbed up the rope, which he did not need but thought appropriate for his greeting on the roof.

"I didn't hear nothing," came the voice from the other side of the ledge. It was the voice of the policeman who had left the room.

"Hi, there," said Remo pleasantly, rising over the ledge. "I'd like to borrow your head for a few minutes."

Blackened hands moved faster than sight. There was a short, wrenching sound on the roof. Then Remo departed through the roof door and scampered down the steps with something in his right hand behind his back, dripping.

When he got to Tomalino's room, he knocked.

A patrolman answered the door.

"What do you want?" asked the patrolman.

"I want to impress upon you and your charge in the room about talking from a pure heart. I think you will agree with me, after few moments of explanation, that truth is the most valuable thing we have."

"Get out of here. We don't need religious nuts."

The door started to close in Remo's face, but something stopped it. The patrolman opened the door again to get a better slam, but something stopped it again. This time he looked to see what the obstruction was. The religious nut in the black suit with the blackened face and blackened feet was holding only one blackened finger in the way, so the patrolman decided to break that finger by slamming the door with the full force of his body.

The door reverberated against his shoulder and the religious nut pushed it open, and shut it behind himself with one hand. Something dripped red from behind the nut's back.

The patrolman went for his gun and the hand did indeed reach the holster. Unfortunately, its wrist connection was rather weak at the time, suffering a cracked bone and a severed nerve. The other patrolman, seeing the speed of the hands, flattened his palms upward.

Vincent "The Blast" Tomalino, a short plug of a man with a stub of a face, begged for mercy.

"No, no."

"I haven't come here to kill you," said Remo. "I have come here to help you speak from a pure heart. All of you sit down on the bed."

When they had done so, Remo lectured them as a school teacher—discussing duty, oaths taken for duty, and an oath that would be taken at a trial shortly where Tomalino would be a witness.

"Purity of heart is most important," Remo said. "The detective who is not here had gone up to the roof to do a bad thing. A very bad thing. The bad thing lacked purity of heart."

The three men eyed the growing red puddle behind the religious nut's back.

"What was this bad thing? I will tell you. He was going to take a payoff for someone to kill you. So were these two other officers."

"The bastards," said Tomalino.

"Judge not lest ye be judged, Mr. Tomalino, for you have been negotiating with your former boss to perhaps not speak with a pure heart."

"No, no. I swear. Never."

"Do not lie," said Remo sweetly. "For this is what happens to people who tell untruths and do not act with purity of heart."

With that, Remo took what he had been holding behind his back, and placed it on Tomalino's lap.

Tomalino's jaw dropped and tears filled his eyes as he went into shock. One of the patrolmen vomited. The other gasped.

"Now, I must ask you to tell an untruth. You will tell no one about this visit, and you two policemen will do your duty, and you, Mr. Tomalino, will speak with a pure heart."

Three heads couldn't nod hard enough. The fourth was beyond nodding and, knowing that the lesson was well-learned, Remo left the room and shut the door behind him.

Down the hotel foyer, three doors down, Remo opened a door he knew would be unlocked. He went to a bathtub that he knew would be filled with water and a special cleansing lotion, then washed his hands and face and feet. As he washed, pods of plastic peeled from his cheeks, changing the contour of his face until now he was almost handsome. He dropped the black pants and shirt into the toilet where, touching water, they dissolved. He heard the police sirens fourteen stories below. He flushed the clothes, emptied the bathtub and went to the closet where a once-worn suit, slightly rumpled as if it had spent a day in the office, hung. He threw it on the bed and opened the bureau drawer where there was a set of underwear, his size; socks, his size; wallet with identification and money; and even a handkerchief. He checked to see if it were clean. Who knew to what extent upstairs would go to assure secrecy?

Remo opened the wallet and checked the wax paper seals. If they were broken he was to discard the identification and say—if he were stopped for questioning—that he had lost his wallet, referring all inquiries about him to a firm in Tacoma, Washington. Should this be done there would be a reference from that firm that, indeed, a Remo Van Sluyters worked for the Busby and Berkley Tool and Die.

Remo opened the seals with his thumb. He looked at the driver's license. He was Remo Horvath and his card said he worked for the fund-raising firm of Jones, Raymond, Winter and Klein.

He checked the closet for his shoes. The ding-dongs upstairs had unloaded well-used cordovans on him again.

As he dressed, he mused over the morning's headlines.

HERO COP GIVES LIFE TO SAVE INFORMER.
Or
MANIAC AX WIELDER ATTACKS HERO COP.
Or
A BLOODY MISS AT TOMALINO.

He walked out into the foyer which was now a confusion of blue uniforms, many of them with brass insignia on the shoulders.

"What happened, officer? What happened?"
"Stay in your room. No one's leaving the building."
"I beg your pardon."

An officer with a broken wrist limped out of Tomalino's room. Why a limp, Remo would never understand. Yet injured people, when they knew they were being observed, often limped.

"We're holding people for questioning," said the higher ranking officer, who looked at the injured patrolman. The patrolman shook his head, which meant to Remo that there was no identification of him as the killer.

But there was a brief interrogation nevertheless. No, Remo had not seen anything or heard anything and what right did the police have questioning him?

"A witness was almost killed tonight and one officer was," the interrogating officer said. "Right next to you."

"Goodness gracious," said Remo and then, turning to anger, he demanded to know what right the police had to keep witnesses in hotels where ordinary citizens stayed hoping to be safe. What was wrong with the jails?

The officer couldn't wait to end the unproductive questioning.

Remo left the hotel complaining about violence, crime in the streets and safety for the average citizen. He could not walk underneath the Tomalino wondow, however, for that was cordoned off by police barricades. A large mound was in the barricaded area. It was covered by a sheet.

One precaution Remo did not take. He did not bother to wipe his prints off the objects in the room he used for changing. There was no need. Police couldn't check out his fingerprints, least of all with the FBI file. Nobody cross-referenced the prints of men who were certifiably dead.

CHAPTER THREE

In answering questions of the Washington press corps, the presidential press secretary appeared serious, yet unworried. Of course, the charges were serious and they would be looked into thoroughly by the Justice Department. No, this was not another Watergate, the press secretary said. He said that with a crisp smile. Any other questions?

"Yeah," replied one reporter, rising. "The incumbents in Miami Beach are charging that your government has been attempting to frame them."

"That was not a charge nationally," said the press secretary.

"It may well become one. They say they have indications that an organization called the Greater Florida Betterment League was just a front for secret and illegal government investigations, including wiretaps and bugging."

"The Justice Department will look into that."

The reporter would not sit down. "This morning, when the local sheriff's office broke into the League headquarters in Miami Beach, they found records leading to the National Betterment League's offices in Kansas City, Missouri. That place turns out to be financed by a U.S. government educational grant. This educational grant doesn't appear to educate many people, but it managed to spend over a million dollars in Miami Beach alone last year. Now what does that mean?"

"It means that will be looked into also."

"Another thing. There's the possibility that this country goes around murdering its citizens. An employee of the Greater Florida Betterment League, one James Bullingsworth, was found dead with an ice pick in his ear. According to Miami Beach officials, he had been seen previously with a notebook saying he was going to become the political kingpin of the city. What do you have to say about that?"

"Same as to everything else. We most certainly are going to look into this. That is, the Justice Department will uncover everything."

"The Justice Department is involved in this thing, according to the charges of the administration in Miami Beach."

"The local government of a minor Florida city is not the major concern of the White House," the secretary said, unable to keep the edge out of his voice.

"And what is this secret organization called Folcroft?" the reporter asked. "Apparently it was behind the whole scheme."

"Gentlemen, this is leading us nowhere. The Justice Department is investigating. You know where to reach the attorney general."

"It's not the where of reaching, but the who of reaching," cracked the reporter, and the press corps broke up in laughter.

The press secretary smiled wanly.

In the Oval Room of the White House, the President watched the press conference live on television. When the reporter mentioned the word "Folcroft," the President's face became ashen.

"Do we have anything like that, Mr. President?" said a trusted aide.

"What?" said the President.

"An organization called Folcroft."

"There is no organization called Folcroft that I know of," said the President. And, technically, he was telling the truth.

Several hundred miles away on the Long Island

Sound, in a sanitarium called Folcroft, one of the social researchers heard the name mentioned on radio and wondered out loud if "we have anything to do with that mess in Miami Beach?" He was assured by his colleagues that this was impossible and they must be talking about some other Folcroft, not the Folcroft Sanitarium famous for its research in changing social patterns and their psychological influence upon the individual in an urban-agricultural environment.

"But wasn't that Kansas City educational grant one of ours?" he asked.

"I'm not sure," said a colleague. "Why don't you ask Dr. Smith?"

And when the researcher heard the name of the director of the Folcroft Sanitarium and thought of that thin, parsimonious gentleman, he was forced to smile.

"No," he admitted. "We couldn't have anything to do with that Miami Beach mess. Could you imagine Dr. Smith involved in anything like that?" And they all laughed for it was known that Dr. Harold W. Smith did not approve of off-color jokes or misspending of a penny, much less political espionage.

Dr. Smith did not eat lunch in the Sanitarium cafeteria that day and his prune-whip yogurt with lemon topping sat unclaimed by any of the other staff. Ordinarily, untouched yogurt would be discarded at the end of the day, but the kitchen help was instructed to save his cup, for Dr. Smith would eat it the next day. It was in the kitchen that he was known to give his sternest lectures on *waste not, want not*. It was also in the kitchen, usually after a salary raise had been denied, that the kitchen help prepared the prune-whip yogurt with liberal dashes of spit.

They would then steal gleeful looks as *waste not, want not* Smith ate his lunch. Had they known the forces the stuffy gentleman commanded, the saliva would have dried in their mouths.

Dr. Smith was not having lunch. The door of his office was locked with instructions to his secretary that he would see no one. Dr. Smith was busy waiting for a telephone to ring. At this stage, there was nothing more to do.

He looked through the one-way glass windows out at the Long Island Sound. He had sailed there several times in the sunshine. From the Sound, his windows looked like giant bright reflectors. A friend had asked him why his windows shone so brightly and his answer was that at Folcroft, we know how to keep them properly cleaned. He wondered if the next tenants would replace them with two-way glass.

Smith sighed. What had gone wrong? There were so many breaks in the chain, no one should have been able to put it together, but here were these cheap politicians in Miami Beach announcing CURE's activities like so many weather forecasts.

How did it happen? Miami Beach had been their breakthrough. For over two years, CURE had been drawing in raw reports from FBI agents; CIA agents; agricultural, postal, IRS and SEC investigators, and feeding them into a computer, programmed to collate and interpret them, and then sending its conclusions on to Kansas City in code. No one should have known, but he realized what had happened.

Smith had become careless. He had failed to build into the system an automatic destruction of the computer printouts and someone had filed them, then someone had gone through them and pierced the code.

Smith sighed again. CURE had lost something important. It had been zeroing in on Miami Beach because it had learned that it would become the nation's new gateway for drug imports. It had planned to let the incumbents win the upcoming municipal election, and then wipe them all out in a flood of indictments. In the ensuing power vacuum it would install new leadership of its own choosing who could close the narcotics pipeline. Now that opportunity was lost.

But more important was the danger that CURE would be unmasked. That would be the greater loss.

For more than a decade now, CURE had been secretly assisting overworked prosecutors, making sure bribed officials were exposed, when ordinarily their corruption would have meant for them a life income, not a life sentence. CURE made sure that men untouchable by the law, suddenly became touched very hard and very thoroughly.

And what could not be handled under the law was handled by CURE in other ways.

Those were the orders of a long-dead president to Smith more than a decade before. Besieged by crime, internal corruption, the threat of revolutionary anarchy, the president had created CURE, a government agency which did not exist, and since it did not exist, was not bound by constitutional safeguards. He had told Smith to head it and to fight crime. That was its mission. To safeguard the country, the president had specified that not even the president could give CURE orders. With one exception. The president could order it to disband.

Smith had worked that out well. There were special funds of which the president knew, whose drying up would dry up CURE. That was only an extra safeguard. Smith, of course, would disband CURE himself any time he was ordered. In fact, several times he had come close, even without orders, when he felt the organization faced exposure.

For exposure was the one big flaw in the entire operation. And now, again, CURE faced exposure.

Dr. Smith looked out at the sound and then back at the computer terminal on his desk.

A red phone buzzed on his desk. That was the call. Smith picked up the phone.

"Yes, sir," he said into the receiver.

"Was that thing in Miami Beach your people?" came the voice.

"Yes, Mr. President."

"Well, it's close. You going to close shop?"

"Are you ordering it, sir?"

"You know where the egg yolk is going to land, don't you? Right on my face."

"For awhile sir, yes. Do you want to give the order?"

"I don't know. This country needs you people, but not as a public agency. What do you recommend?"

"We've begun closing down, sort of a self-induced dormancy. This line will disconnect by 7 p.m. The Network of grants that supports us is already being cut loose. Fortunately, none of the other Betterment League offices around the country were operational. Only Miami Beach. The computers there are erasing themselves. They've been doing it selectively for the last day. We'll be ready to disappear at a moment's notice."

"And that special person?"

"I haven't spoken to him yet."

"You could transfer him into some government operation. Definitely military operation."

"No, sir, I'm sorry. I cannot do that."

"What will you do with him?"

"I had planned to eliminate him in a situation like this. You don't want him walking the streets uncontrolled."

"Had planned?"

Smith sighed. "Yes sir. When it was possible."

"You mean he can't be killed?"

"No sir. Of course, he can be killed, but God help anyone or anything that misses."

There was a silence. A long silence.

"You've got a week," the president said. "Settle this thing or disband. I'm leaving tomorrow for Vienna, and I'll be gone a week. The heat won't really build up until

I get back. So you can use that week. Settle it or disband. How can I reach you after this line is dead?"

"You can't."

"What should I do with the phone?"

"Nothing. Put it back in your bureau drawer. After 7 p.m. tonight, it will be your direct line to the White House gardener."

"Then how will I know?" the president asked.

"We have a week," Smith said. "If we clean it up, I'll contact you. If we do not . . . well, it was an honor to serve with you."

There was a pause on the other end of the line.

"Goodbye and good luck, Smith."

"Thank you, sir."

Dr. Harold W. Smith, director of the Folcroft Sanitarium in Rye, New York, returned the receiver to the cradle. He would need the offered luck, for in a week the most important of all links would be destroyed—himself. That came with the job. He would not be the first to shed his blood for his country, nor would he be the last.

The intercom buzzed nervously. Smith opened a line.

"I told you I didn't want to be disturbed," he said.

"Two FBI men out here, Dr. Smith. They want to speak to you."

"In a minute," said Smith. "Tell them I'll be with them in a minute."

Well, the investigation had begun. CURE's compromise was well underway. He picked up another phone and dialed through an open line to a ski resort in Vermont, closed for the off-season.

When the phone was answered at the other end, Smith said somberly: "Hello, Aunt Mildred."

"No Mildred here."

"I'm sorry. I'm very sorry. I must have the very wrong number."

"That's okay."

33

"Yes. A very wrong number," said Smith, and wanted to say more, but he no longer had any guarantee that this line was not already being tapped.

For all practical purposes, he had said it all. The last hope of CURE, that special person, knew now there was a "condition red."

What Smith had wanted to say was, "Remo, you're our only chance. If you've ever come through before, you've got to come through now." Maybe the tone of his voice carried that plea. Then again, maybe it didn't, for Smith could have sworn he heard laughing at the other end of the line.

CHAPTER FOUR

"Free at last, free at last. Thank God almighty, free at last."

Remo Williams returned the phone to the cradle and danced out of his lodge room onto the empty carpeted foyer that a few months earlier had suffered the constant tromping of ski boots. Now it supported the bare, dancing feet of one very happy man.

"Free at last," he sang. "Free at last." He danced down the steps, taking them not three at a time or four at a time, but all at a time, one leap like a cat and landing spinning.

But for his thick wrists, he appeared a very average man, somewhere near six feet, somewhere near average weight, deep brown eyes and high cheekbones—the plastic surgeon, by accident, returning them to almost what they looked like ten years earlier, before all this.

He pirouetted into the lodge lounging room where a frail Oriental sat in a golden kimono, his legs crossed in lotus position before a television set.

The Oriental's face was as silent as glass, not even the wisp of a beard moved, not even the eyes blinked. He, too, looked like an ordinary man—an old, very old Korean.

Remo glanced at the set to make sure a commercial was playing. When he saw the soapsuds filling a tub and a woman being congratulated by her peers for a cleaner wash, he danced before the television screen.

"Free at last," he sang. "Free at last."

"Only a fool is free," said the Oriental. "And he, only from wisdom."

"Free, Little Father. Free."

"When a fool is happy, wise men shudder."

"Free. F. R. E. E. Eeeeeeeee! Free."

Noticing that the commercial was fading into the storyline of *As the Planet Revolves,* Remo quickly removed himself from the viewing line of Chiun, the latest Master of Sinanju. For when American soap operas appeared on the screen, no one was allowed to disturb his pleasure.

Barefoot, Remo danced out into the spring mud of the Vermont countryside, delirious with joy. It was a "condition red," and his instructions were burned into his mind by his ten years of waiting, since he had gotten his very first assignment.

The bastards had just recruited him then, a Newark policeman, an orphan with no close friends who would miss him. They framed him for murder and sent him to an electric chair that didn't work. When he woke, they told him they were an organization that didn't exist; that now he was their enforcement arm who also didn't exist, because he had just died in the electric chair. And just in case he should happen to bump into someone who knew him when, they changed his face and kept changing it periodically.

"Condition red," Smith had said, before Remo left on his first mission, "is the most important instruction I give you."

Remo had listened quietly. He had known just what he was going to do when he left Folcroft that first time. He would make a half-hearted attempt at the hit and then disappear. It didn't work out that way, but that was what he had planned.

"Condition red means," Smith had said, "that CURE has been compromised. It means that we are disbanding. For you, condition red means you should remove the compromise if possible. If not, run and don't try to reach us."

"Run and don't try to reach you," said Remo, humoring the man.

"Or remove the compromise."

"Or remove the compromise," Remo repeated dutifully.

"Now chances are I won't be able to communicate with you under those conditions, at least not safely. So the code for condition red is calling you, asking for Aunt Mildred, and then saying I must have a very wrong number. Do you understand?"

"Aunt Mildred," Remo repeated. "Got it."

"When you hear my voice asking for Aunt Mildred, you become the last hope of CURE," Smith said.

"Right," Remo said. "Last hope." He wanted to get out of Folcroft and vanish. To hell with Smith, to hell with CURE, to hell with everybody.

It never worked that way. It turned into a new life. Years went by. Names on lists, people he didn't know, people who thought that guns were protection and suddenly found those guns in their mouths. Years of training—under Chiun, the Master of Sinanju—who slowly changed Remo's body, mind and nervous system into something more than human: a man of years without tomorrows because when you change your name and your place of living and even your face often enough you stop making plans.

So it was over now and Remo danced in the sunshine. The air was good and clean; the new buds were fragrant on the hill. A young girl and her dog were standing by the silent chairlift being put into seasonal retirement. Vermont labor being what it was, the project was two months behind schedule.

In all of industrious New England, Vermont somehow has escaped the Protestant work ethic. People buying homes and land in this beautiful state find it almost impossible to get a plumber or an electrician to do a fast job. Land waits for houses and houses wait for service and the whole state works off a tax base that would shame a Polynesian island.

But that was not Remo's problem either, nor was secrecy about so many things anymore.

"Hello," said the little girl. "My dog's name is Puffin and mine is Nora and I have a brother J. P. and Timmy and an Aunt Geri, what's yours?"

"My aunt?"

"No, your name," said Nora.

"Remo. Remo Williams," said Remo who had been Remo Pelham and Remo Barry and Remo Bednick and Remo so many things, but now he was Remo Williams again and that was his name and it felt good in the saying of it. "Remo Williams. Do you want to see something amazing nobody else can do in the whole wide world, except a very few people from a far-off land?"

"Possibly," said Nora.

"I can run up that chairlift."

"That's silly," Nora said. "So can I. Anybody can run up the hill."

"No. On the lines, right up over the chairs, along that steel band that goes from support to support."

"You cannot. Nobody can do that."

"I can do it," said Remo. "You watch."

And he ran to a silent empty chair and with a leap was one hand on it, and without breaking motion, pulled himself above it and onto the wire.

Nora laughed and clapped, and then Remo ran upward, keeping the balance of his body centered, his bare feet hardly touching the metal, hot in the late spring sun.

It was not training, not as Chiun would call it training, because he was not using his mind, focusing his forces. Rather he was showing off for a little girl and just running, running upward, over a little depression in the ground that put him 45 feet above it, over the chair hooks to the wire, up to the top of the mountain, and when he got there, he stood surveying the now-green ski slopes, the other mountains rising green into the blue sky. He could if he wished buy a home right there. Or even the whole mountain. Or even an island somewhere and throw coconuts for the rest of his life.

He was, as few men were, free. Whatever had caused the condition red was Smith's problem and not his. So Smitty would probably take his own life. So what? Smitty knew what he had volunteered for. He bought the package. And that was the difference. Remo had never volunteered. Maybe he would return to Newark, which had been placed off limits to him when he was dragged aboard CURE's ship of fools. Maybe he would see what Newark was like. So many years.

He thought about Smith again and then forced the thought from his mind. Smitty had volunteered and Remo hadn't and that was that. He wasn't going to give it one more thought. Not one.

He thought about how he wasn't going to think about it, all the way down the wire, past the clapping little girl whom he ignored and into the lodge. He waited, dandling his leg nervously, while *As the Planet Revolves* moved into *Dr. Lawrence Walters, Psychiatrist at Large,* and various other daytime dramas where nothing ever happened but all the actors discussed the action. Remo had long ago attributed Chiun's liking of the soap operas to the first warning signal of senility. To which Chiun had replied that in all the crassness of America, it had produced one great art form and this was it, and that if Remo were Korean, he could appreciate beauty, but since Remo could not appreciate anything, not even the most valuable training in the history of mankind, how could he appreciate something as fine as a soap opera?

So Remo steamed as Dr. Carrington Blake explained to Willa Douglaston that her son, Bertram, faced a possible problem with Quaalude. Bertram, as Remo remembered from years past, had faced a problem first with marijuana, then with heroin, and then with cocaine, and now since Quaaludes were in, it was Quaaludes.

During one commercial, Chiun commented:

"See an ungrateful son."

Remo did not respond. What he had to say required more time than a mere commercial.

When the last show was to be continued and when Chiun turned from the set, Remo exploded.

"I couldn't care less what happened to Smith or the organization, Little Father. I couldn't care less. I don't care," Remo yelled. "You know what?"

Chiun sat silently.

"You know what, Little Father?" Remo yelled angrily. "You know what?"

Chiun nodded.

"I'm happy," screamed Remo. "Happy, happy, happy."

"I am glad you are happy, Remo. Because if you are happy now, I would be most feared to see you when you were unhappy."

"I'm free now."

"Something has happened?" asked Chiun.

"Right. The organization is coming apart," Remo said. Chiun, he knew, had a vague understanding of CURE, vague to a large degree because CURE fulfilled the basic requirement of Chiun's services by paying regularly, and after that it meant little to Chiun what CURE really did. He called it "the emperor" because it was the tradition of the House of Sinanju to serve emperors.

"Then we will find another emperor to serve," Chiun said. "See now my wisdom. Because we have faithfully served one, we always have employment in the future."

"I don't want to work for anyone else," said Remo.

Korean mutterings emanated from Chiun's mouth and Remo knew they were not complete sentences, just minor curses, a few of which he recognized such as "White man," "pigeon droppings," and something that could only be translated into English as "rotted bellies of untamed pigs." There was, of course, the traditional casting of jewels into mud and the inability of even a Master of Sinanju to transform rice husks into a banquet.

"And of your training, what of that?" Chiun said. "Of the years given you that have never been given to white men before? What of that? You have, I must confess, in all your training, made an adequate beginning. Yes, I will say it. Adequate. You have achieved adequacy . . . for a beginner."

"Thank you, Little Father," Remo said. "But you've never really understood why I do these things."

"Understood, yes. Appreciated, no. You say patriotism, love of country. But who has given you the secrets of Sinanju—America or the Master of Sinanju?"

"America paid for it."

"They paid money and for that I could have given you the master of Kung Fu, Aiki and Karate. They would not have known the difference. They would have thought how wonderful he can break bricks with his hands and arms and kick things with his feet. These are mere games compared to Sinanju. You know that well."

"Yes, I do, Little Father."

"We are assassins; these people are little dancers."

"I know that."

"Dr. Smith would have been delighted with a dancer, but I gave you Sinanju, to a white man I gave it honestly, and made even the walls of stone but powder in the wind before your steps. These things—I, Master of Sinanju, gave you."

"Yes, Little Father."

"And now you throw them aside like so much old clothing."

"I will never forget what you have . . ."

"Forget. How dare you say you will not forget? Have you learned nothing? Each day you fail to remember, you forget. Knowing is not a question of not forgetting, it is a question of remembering with your body, with your mind and with your very nerves. That which is not remembered every moment is lost."

"Little Father, I don't want to kill any more."

Stricken with the statement, Chiun was silent for a moment, and Remo knew he could get the full treatment of the benevolent master and the ungrateful student. He would get the history of Sinanju, how this poor village, unable to support itself, rented its assassins out to the emperors of China, and how if a Master of Sinanju failed, the babies of the village would be drowned, because drowning was better than starving. It was called sending the babies home and Remo had heard it countless times. It came down to whether you killed your assignments or the innocent babies of Sinanju.

Remo heard it all and when Chiun was finished, he said:

"I don't like to kill people, Little Father. Not really, not always and not often."

"Drivel," said Chiun. "Who likes to kill? Does a surgeon like or dislike a liver? Does one of your mechanics like or dislike a motor? Of course not. And I would just as soon sit in peace with the world and give love to one and all who passed."

"That's hard to believe, Chiun. I mean, what with what happens to anyone interrupting your shows and everything, know what I mean."

"I am not discussing my meager pleasures," said Chiun angrily. Remo knew that when Chiun was imagining himself as a sweet, delicate blossom, to remind him that he was the world's most deadly assassin was a breach of etiquette.

"I too would like never to raise my hand again," Chiun said. "But this cannot be so, and so I do what every man should do. His job as well as he can. That is what I do."

"We'll never agree, Little Father. Not on that."

And the matter appeared decided, until a late night newscast where Remo saw why the condition red. He watched the reporter question the Presidential aide, and when the word Folcroft came up, Remo became hysterical.

"I wish I could have seen Smitty's face when he heard that," said Remo laughing. But he did not laugh long for he did see the face of Dr. Harold W. Smith. Television cameras had been denied admittance to the grounds of Folcroft Sanitarium but a telephoto lens had captured a look at Dr. Smith as he walked, hands behind his back, toward the waters of Long Island Sound. His face was his usual mask of calm, but Remo knew that underneath it was a great sadness. And seeing the head of CURE weak and helpless like that, Remo felt a rage he never knew he possessed. It was all right for him to hate, possibly even to verbally abuse Smith, but he didn't like to see anyone else do it, particularly a country which would never know the debt it owed to Smith. He watched the TV set until Smith vanished behind the back of the sanitarium's main building.

Then he called out: "Chiun, I want to talk to you about something. I've got a little surprise for you."

"I am already packed," said the Master of Sinanju. "What took you so long to change your mind?"

CHAPTER FIVE

Getting off the plaine at the Dade County Airport was like walking into a hot towel.

"Eccchhh," said Remo but Chiun said not a word. He had made it clear that so long as Remo got him to a television set by 11:30 a.m., he did not care where they stayed or how they travelled. He did not like to talk before his shows.

Remo carried all his clothes in a fat attaché case. For Chiun, they had to wait at a luggage wheel inside the airport. A chute vomited the luggage contents of each plane onto a revolving belt, around which passengers stood, waiting, looking for their suitcases and boxes and packages.

In the general jostle at the luggage wheel, Chiun made his way to the lip of the revolving belt, and although he looked like a frail feather in a herd of cattle, nevertheless he managed neither to be pushed aside nor ignored.

"Who's helping that poor old man?" asked a hefty woman with a Bronx accent.

"It is all right," said Chiun. "I will manage."

"He doesn't need your help, lady," said Remo. "Don't fall for it."

"That is my strong young son who makes aged father bear heavy burdens," Chiun confided to the woman.

"He doesn't look like you," said the woman.

"Adopted," whispered Chiun.

A large red lacquered trunk with shiny brass trimmings came forth from the chute.

"That is ours," said Chiun to the woman.

"Hey, you. You gonna help your father with the luggage?" the woman cried out angrily.

Remo shook his head. "No. But you will." He turned his back on the luggage wheel and strolled to a newsstand and it was here that he realized how much he had come to rely upon CURE in his assignments.

There would be no reports waiting for him on who was where or doing what or who was vulnerable because of something in his past. There would be no new name with new credit cards and a secure house. There would be no analysis of the problem by Smith, and as he purchased the two local newspapers, he realized how alone he really was.

The eyes and ears of CURE had been put to sleep. Remo read the headlines. It was now called "The League Affair."

What Remo gathered from the newspapers was that somehow, notes on what the Greater Florida Betterment League had really been doing had gotten into the hands of a minor local politician, a functionary in the election bureau. He was making all the charges.

According to the local politician, the secret notes proved that a secret organization called Folcroft was conducting political espionage in Miami Beach. The espionage was financed by the federal government and its goal was to indict the mayor and current city administration.

"Worse than Watergate," said the local politician who said he had access to the secret notes and would release them at the proper time. The politician's name was Willard Farger.

Remo put down the papers. All he knew was that the papers had printed that a lot of people said a lot of things. There was no scale of verification, no scale of probability, none of the intensive checks and counterchecks that had gone into the knowing of something. What did he really know?

That a Willard Farger, who was a political cohort of the present administration, had said a lot of things and probably had access to the notes compromising CURE. Remo shrugged. It was a good enough beginning.

He picked up the paper again. A League employee had been murdered. The sheriff did not deny that it could be Folcroft agents. There was an editorial. "Government by Assassins?"

Remo would have to show that one to Chiun, who had once reasoned that the ideal form of government was that where the ablest assassin ruled. Remo smiled. The Master of Sinanju, in his governmental philosophy, was not unlike businessmen who believed government should be run by businessmen, or social workers who believed governments should be run as a social program, or generals who thought that military men made the best presidents, or even like the philosopher Plato who, while outlining the ideal form of government, said its leader should be, surprise, surprise, "a philosopher king."

Willard Farger, thought Remo, if you have ever talked in your political career, you will talk to me. You're a good beginning. Remo folded the papers under his arm. If CURE were still working, he could have had press identification if he wanted.

"Hello, Mr. Farger, I want to interview you." *Wham. Bam.*

Press identification. Remo mulled the thought, and discarded immediately his first idea of a pre-dawn approach to Farger's bedroom. Farger himself would be deluged with reporters. He looked at the paper again. On Page 7, there was a picture. The Farger family at home. And there was pudgy-faced Mrs. Farger, sucking in her cheeks and angling in at the camera to look slimmer, leaning forward, in front of her husband. In front of him, Remo thought. The way to Willard Farger, he realized, would be through Mrs. Farger.

Remo threw the papers into a waste basket and

looked over to the luggage wheel. Sure enough, five vacationers were sweating and groaning under the large trunks which contained Chiun's kimonos; his television taping machine; his sleeping mat; his autographed picture of Rad Rex, star of *As the Planet Revolves;* his special rice. In all there were 157 kimonos and six trunks. Remo had told Chiun to pack light.

The hefty woman, perspiring under one of the trunks, said to a young boy: "That's him. That's the old man's adopted son. Won't even help the old man after all the old man has done for him."

She put down the trunk.

"Animal," she yelled at Remo. "Ungrateful animal. Look at him, everyone. The animal who would make his aged father do heavy lifting. C'mon over and see the animal."

Remo smiled pleasantly for one and all.

"The animal. Look at him," said the woman, pointing to Remo. Chiun stood off to the side, innocent of the commotion, a mere aged Korean hoping to enjoy the golden years of his life. Chiun could have, if he had wished, taken the trunks and the volunteer porters to boot and hurled them all back up the luggage ramp. But Chiun considered carrying things to be "Chinamen's work", meaning work unworthy of a Korean. It was for Chinese or whites or blacks.

He had once complained that Japanese did not like to carry things because of arrogance. When Remo had pointed out that Chiun was not known to like lifting, Chiun had responded that there was a difference between the Korean and Japanese attitudes.

"Japanese are arrogant. They *think* the work is beneath them. Koreans are not arrogant. We *know* the work is beneath us."

Now Chiun had a gaggle of tourists doing Chinamen's work.

"C'mon over here, sonny, and help your father," yelled the woman

Remo shook his head

"C'mon, lazy bastard," joined in other volunteer porters

Remo shook his head again.

"You animal "

At this, Chiun shuffled to center stage just a bit more slowly than usual. He raised his thin hands, the long fingernails pointing upward as if in prayer.

"You are good people," he said. "So good and kind and thoughtful. So you not realize that everyone is not so good as you, that their decency is not so great, that it can never be as great You are angry because my adopted son does not share your goodness. But you do not realize that some people from birth are denied this goodness. I have tried so hard to teach him, yet for a flower to grow from the seed, that seed must be planted in good soil. It is my great sadness that my son is rocky soil. Do not yell at him. He is incapable of your goodness."

"Thanks, Little Father," said Remo

"Animal. I knew it. He's an animal," snarled the woman. Turning to her husband, a giant of a man that Remo estimated at six-feet-five, 325 pounds, the woman said, "Marvin, teach the animal some decency."

"Ethel," said the gigantic Marvin, in a surprisingly timid voice, "If he doesn't want to help his old man, that's his business "

"Marvin. How could you let that animal get away with what he's doing to this sweet, old, preciously lovely *mensch?*"

Ethel, overcome by warmth, dashed to Chiun and hugged him to her overly ample bosom. "A *mensch*. A pure *mensch*. Marvin, teach the animal some manners."

"He's half my size, Ethel. Come on."

"I'm not leaving this poor soul with that animal, Marvin. What an ungrateful son."

Marvin sighed and Remo watched him approach. He would not hit him hard. Maybe just take the wind out of him.

Remo looked up at Marvin. Marvin looked down at Remo.

"Hit the animal," yelled Ethel, clasping the world's deadliest assassin to her chest, while her husband faced the second deadliest.

"Look, buddy," said Marvin softly, reaching into his pocket. "I don't want to get into your family business, know what I mean?"

"Are you going to hit him or are you going to talk?" yelled Ethel

"You are such a sensitive woman," said Chiun, who knew that gross-sized people liked to be called sensitive because they were called that so rarely.

"Break his head or I will," yelled Ethel, hugging tighter her precious bundle.

Marvin pulled out of his pocket some bills, which was probably the luckiest thing his hand had ever done for itself.

"Here's twenty bucks. Help your old man with his suitcases."

"I won't," said Remo. "You don't know him and you're not the first he's hornswoggled into doing his heavy lifting. So put away your money."

"Look, buddy, it's my family problem now. Help him with the suitcases, will ya?"

"If you don't slam that animal right now, Marvin, you'll never know my bed again."

Remo watched Marvin's face light up in joyous surprise.

"Is that a promise, Ethel?"

Remo saw this as a good opportunity to disengage, but Chiun, ever the gallant, said to the woman: "He is unworthy of you, precious flower."

The precious flower had always known this and putting Chiun down, she hurled herself at her brute of a husband, slamming his head with her pocketbook.

Remo ducked out of the way and left them squabbling with a crowd forming to watch the family fight.

"Proud of yourself, Chiun?" asked Remo.

"I brought happiness into her life."

"Next time, get a porter."

"There were none to be found right away."

"Did you look?"

"People who do Chinamen's work should look for me, not me for them."

"I'll be out tonight. I've got some work," said Remo. "Where are our quarters?"

Remo looked astonished. "I forgot that," he said.

"Ah," said Chiun. "See how valuable an emperor can be?"

Chiun was right of course. But what he did not realize was that their "emperor"—CURE— was in danger of being destroyed and only Remo could save it. If—and it was a big "if"—if he could straighten out the mess of the "The League Affair."

CHAPTER SIX

Willard Farger, fourth deputy assistant commissioner of elections, woke up with the first rays of sun glinting from his swimming pool into his bedroom, the telephone receiver whining away. It had been taken from its cradle so he could get a night's sleep. Willard Farger couldn't be bothered by just any reporter anymore.

It had taken him exactly one hour and fifteen minutes, or approximately his third interview with the press several days before, to forget how he would formerly hound reporters to include his name in stories about picnics, Boy Scout festivals and party fund-raising suppers.

Then he would personally deliver press releases from party headquarters, try to tell jokes to anyone in the city rooms of the *Miami Beach Dispatch* and the *Miami Beach Journal,* and excitedly await the next edition home or office.

Sometimes on a slow news day, he would get: "Also in attendance was Willard Farger, fourth deputy assistant-commissioner of elections." On those days, he would ask his colleagues at the county administration building if they had read the papers that day. He would wait around the press room to see if reporters wanted anyone to go out for sandwiches, and he never passed up a chance to buy a reporter a drink at a bar.

These chances did not come often, since reporters thought of him as a publicity hound and a nuisance. To be bought a drink by Willard Farger, fourth deputy assistant-commissioner of elections, meant you had to speak with him while downing it, and possibly longer.

With one television press conference, all this changed. Willard Farger now stood against the government with "proof of the most insidious danger to our freedoms in the history of the nation." He was news, growing national news, and only at the insistence of his political bosses did he begin to talk to reporters from the local papers. After all, hadn't he made the front page of the *New York Times*?

"You can't ignore the *Dispatch* and the *Journal*," the sheriff had told him.

Secretly Farger suspected the sheriff was jealous. Did the *Washington Post* ever do a profile on a mere Dade County sheriff?

"I can't localize my image either," Farger had said. "In one two-minute network newscast, I reach twenty-one percent of all the voters in the nation. Twenty one percent. What do I get from the *Dispatch* and the *Journal*, a fiftieth of one percent?"

"But you live in Miami Beach, Bill."

"And Abraham Lincoln lived in Springfield. So what?"

"Bill, you're not president of the United States. You're just another guy who's trying to re-elect Tim Cartwright as mayor next week. So I think you'd better talk to the *Dispatch* and the *Journal*."

"I think it's my business, not yours, Sheriff," said Willard Farger, who a week earlier had offered to sweep out the sheriff's garage and had been refused, because it might be construed as using public employees for personal purposes.

Sheriff Clyde McAdow had thrown up his hands, given a last warning that when the national reporters left, the *Dispatch* and *Journal* would still be in Miami Beach, and all of this reached Willard Farger not at all.

Men who were on national television did not go taking advice from local sheriffs. Willard Farger kept the telephone off the hook so that local reporters couldn't reach him. He would have to get an unlisted telephone, he thought as he rolled out of bed. Maybe send the number to the presidents of CBS, NBC and ABC. Perhaps *Time* and *Newsweek* also. He couldn't leave out the *New York Times* or the *Washington Post* either, even though their circulations nationally were not as heavy as the magazines. Important in the intellectual communities, however.

Farger yawned and shuffled into the bathroom. He blinked his eyes and rubbed his face, a somewhat fleshy face with a bulbous nose and small blue eyes, topped by a good head of gray hair, which he thought gave the impression of strength and wisdom and dignity.

He looked into the mirror that morning and liked what he saw.

"Good morning, governor," he said, and by the time he was finished shaving, he was—in his mind—conducting cabinet meetings in the White House.

"Have a good day, Mr. President," he said, applying the stinging after shave lotion.

He bathed, then hot-combed his hair, mentally toying with the idea of a united world, free of war and strife, where every man could sit under his fig tree and be at peace.

He put on his gray worsted that morning, a television blue shirt, and when he sat down to breakfast, his wife Laura, still in curlers, put an envelope on his plate instead of soft-boiled two-minute eggs.

"What's this?" asked Farber.

"Open it," said his wife.

"Where are my eggs?"

"Open it."

So Willard Farger tore the end off the fat envelope and saw tightly compressed bills in it. He pulled them out slowly and was surprised to see that they were twenty-dollar bills. Thirty of them.

"This is six hundred dollars, Laura," he said. "Six

hundred dollars. Not a bribe, is it? I can't have my career ruined by a measly six hundred dollar bribe."

Laura Farger, who had seen her husband gratefully accept five dollars to fix a ticket, cocked a disdainful eyebrow.

"It's not a bribe. It's mine. It was given to me for a magazine interview."

"Without checking with me? You don't know how to handle reporters, Laura. You know nothing of the intricacies and the traps of the media. For a crummy six hundred dollars, you may have damaged my career. What did you tell the magazine?"

"I told them you were a wonderful husband, a good family man, and that you loved dogs and children."

Farger pondered that statement for a moment.

"Good. That was all right. Did you tell him anything else?"

"No. Just that I'd speak to you. He wants to interview you."

"What magazine?"

"I forget."

"You give an interview to a magazine and forget? Laura, how could you do this to me? Just as my career is taking off. An amateur handling the media is the most dangerous thing for a political career. Politics, Laura, is for pros, not housewives."

"He said he'd pay $6,000 for an interview with you."

"Cash?" said Willard Farger.

"Cash," said Laura Farger who knew by the way her husband asked the question that she could count on at least a trip to Europe that year. Six thousand dollars went a long way. "The guy's name who interviewed me was Remo something. I forget his last name."

"Cash," mused Willard Farger.

On a yacht cruising past the famous skyline of Miami Beach, a man who smelled heavily of lilac cologne heard complaints from Sheriff Clyde McAdow; Tim Cartwright, mayor of Miami Beach; and city manager Clyde Moskowitz.

"Farger is becoming impossible," said McAdow. "Impossible."

"Impossible," said Mayor Cartwright.

"Incredibly impossible," said City Manager Moskowitz.

"Idiots usually are," said the man who smelled heavily of lilac cologne. "And you forget that if he were not an idiot, he would not have done what we wished."

"Which was?" Cartwright asked.

"To make himself a target for the people who are trying to send you to jail, Mayor."

"Yeah. But what can they do to him now? Under the glare of all this publicity?"

"Gentlemen, it is going to be a long hot day today and I intend to get some very good sleep. I would suggest you get some sleep also. When you asked my help, you said you would leave everything in my hands. Consider it left. And don't panic if a few more idiots get killed."

The three politicians exchanged glances. Jail after indictment was one thing; murder and killing was something else totally.

"Gentlemen, I see by your faces that you feel somewhat betrayed," said the man with the lilac cologne. He was a squarish sort of man with heavy shoulders and a tubular waist, whose ample bulk made him appear shorter than his six-feet-two. His face had the smooth, unworried look of old wealth; the sort of tan one does not sit on the beach for, but acquires naturally when one lives in Palm Beach, eats breakfast on the patio and yachts extensively.

Now he sat with a towel draped around his waist, lounging in the stateroom of his vessel with three nervous men in business suits.

"Let me ask you a question," the man said. "You blanch at killings It offends you. Does it offend you enough, Mayor Cartwright, that you will return all the millions in graft, the diamonds in safe-deposit boxes, the stocks and bonds in Switzerland?" He ignored Cartwright's open-mouthed stare, and went on. "And you, Sheriff, does it offend you enough to give up your wife's 50 percent interest in the construction company which gets most of the city's building contracts? And to give back the money which helped buy the auto dealership that you list under your brother-in-law's name? And you, Mr. Moskowitz, how much does it offend you? Enough to give back all the money you have taken by adding 10 percent to every city purchase in the last five years?"

He looked at the three men, hard, one after another.

"You are surprised that I know these things," he said. "But you forget. I have the notebook that Bullingsworth compiled and it is only the fact that I have it, and not he, that keeps you three from jail. The price I paid was his death; would you have me give a refund?

"Now the simple fact is that a secret organization of the federal government has been planning for two years to put you all in jail. By following my advice, you have foiled this plan. Publicly exposing the government has made it impossible for the government to act against you. Now this secret organization is making its last attempt against you. And instead of letting you three be the targets, I am using poor, simple Willard Farger as the target. And suddenly you are struck with remorse. It is too late for attacks of conscience. If you wish to stay in office and out of prison, you must do it my way. Because no other way will work."

Mayor Cartwright and Sheriff McAdow were silent, unmoving, but City Manager Moskowitz shook his head vigorously from side to side.

"If they wanted to get us, why not months ago, before Tim's reelection campaign?" he asked.

"For a simple reason," the heavyset man said. "If you were all indicted months ago, there would have been a mad scramble of contenders for your positions. The government's plan was more clever, more insidious. They were going to let you get re-elected, Mayor Cartwright, and then indict you and your whole administration. In the confusion they were going to pick their own man to run the city."

"But now they can't touch me," Cartwright said. "My only opposition in the election next week is that silly ninny, Polaney, And if they try to indict me now, it'll be a scandal. This is going to be bigger than Watergate. We've got them over a barrel."

"Watergate was done by amateurs," the heavyset man said.

"Ex-CIA and FBI men," said Cartwright defensively.

The man shook his head. "When they worked for their former organizations, they worked in a context that made them competent and professional. On their own, they were stumbling, bumbling men taking risks that shouldn't have been taken. No, gentlemen, you underestimate your opponents. You have uncovered a secret organization that has obviously operated effectively for years. Do you expect them now to cut and run? Believe me. What they are doing now is retreating to defensive positions, while they devise a new plan of attack against you. Farger is to be the lightning rod for that attack. That is why the idiot is necessary."

The heavyset man rose from his pillows and walked to a window of his stateroom. He looked at the Miami Beach skyline, money rising out of sand. Cities always had been prizes of war, from the fall of Troy to the Battle of Moscow. To take a city, that was an accomplishment.

Behind him, Moskowitz said: "You didn't tell us it would be this way."

"I didn't tell you the sun would rise either, but what do you expect? To have the cover of darkness forever?" He wheeled and faced them angrily. "Gentlemen, you are at war." He measured the tension in their faces. Good, he thought. They are losing the illusion of safety. Always good for green troops.

"But, don't worry, gentlemen. You are at war, but I am your general. And the first thing I have done is to set Farger out as bait to see what our opponents plan."

"But killing?" said Moskowitz. "I don't like killing."

"I didn't say he would be killed. I said he would be their first target. Now I think the meeting is concluded. I'll have my launch take you back to my city."

"Your city?" asked Mayor Cartwright, but the heavy-set man with the heavy smell of lilac cologne did not hear him. He was intently watching the back of Moskowitz as he stepped out onto the highly varnished deck. Moskowitz was still shaking his head.

CHAPTER SEVEN

Willard Farger wanted to make one thing perfectly clear before the interview began.

"I am not giving your magazine an interview just for the six thousand dollars. I'm giving you this interview so that a broader spectrum of the American public will see the treachery they are pitted against. I want to return America to the principles that made her great. Did you bring the money?"

"After the interview," said Remo. He had noticed the two plainclothesmen outside Farger's home, so he might have to leave with Farger if he couldn't find out what he wanted in the interview.

"I'll be perfectly honest with you," said Farger. "This money is going to go right into Mayor Cartwright's campaign coffers. I'm not going to use a cent of it myself. It's going to pay to elect a mayor with the guts to stand up against an insidious central government. So I'm really taking the money for the people."

"In other words, you want the money up front," Remo said.

"I want the people to be assured of their birthright as Americans."

"I'll give you a thousand up front and the rest after the interview."

"Remo, if I may call you Remo," said Farger, "this is a time of crisis in America, polarization of the races, rich against poor, labor against capital. Good government can bring us back to our senses, but it costs money to elect good government."

"Two thousand up front," Remo said.

"No checks," said Farger, and the interview began.

Remo noted that Farger must have done extensive research into this secret government agency and this Folcroft. How did Farger do it?

Farger answered that every American should be aware of his government in order to help improve it. That was the trouble with government today.

How did Farger find out the Betterment League was a front and how did he get his hands on the Bullingsworth notes?

Farger answered that he was a product of an American home with American values; decent hard-working parents had taught him persistence.

Did Farger still have the Bullingsworth notes and, if so, where did he have them?

"Any man who wants to serve his community must take stock of his resources and apply them in the most judicious and farsighted manner," said Farger.

Who else but Farger knew about the notes?

"Let me make one thing perfectly clear. Morality is the key to everything. The little people of America, of this city where I was born and raised, all of them are with me in standing up and crying out in a single loud voice: Foul."

Remo shrugged. Perhaps reporters knew how to cut through this windage. Maybe they knew special key questions that would unspring direct answers.

"You're not answering my questions," Remo said.

"Which question haven't I answered?" asked Farger innocently.

"All of them," said Remo.

"I never fail to answer a question," Farger said. "America was built by forthright men who answered forthright questions with candor. I am known for my candor."

All right, thought Remo. If that's the way he wants to play it, that's the way we'll play it.

Remo studied Farger's face, peering intently into his eyes, then at his hair. He raised his hands to frame it.

"We need photos for the story. A good cover shot. Front of the magazine."

Farger shaded the angle of his head so Remo could see the better side.

"A background," Remo said. "A background. We need a good background."

"With my family?"

Remo shook his head. "Someplace important. To capture your stature if you know what I mean. Some place which best epitomizes your spirit."

"I'm not going to fly to the White House for just one picture," said Farger angrily.

"I was thinking of some place close to home."

"It's a little late for the governor's mansion, isn't it?"

"Outdoors," said Remo. "A man of the land."

"Do you think so?" asked Farger intently. "I've thought of myself more as the answer to our troubled cities."

"Land and city," said Remo.

Did Remo have an idea for a good background?

He most certainly did.

The plainclothesmen followed the pair in a separate car. They drove down Collins Avenue, Miami Beach's main drag, turned into several side streets, then back to Collins Avenue. The detectives were still following.

"Here?" asked Farger.

"Too rich a background," Remo said. "If you should ever run for office yourself, your opponents could use the picture and smear you as the rich man's candidate."

"Good thinking," Farger said.

"Any roads lead into the countryside?"

"Sure, but we're not on it."

"The countryside," said Remo, and Farger wheeled the car around while the detectives wheeled their car around.

"Stop the car," said Remo.

"This isn't the countryside."

"I know, just stop the car." Farger slowed his car and parked at a curb. The unmarked police car stopped also.

Remo got out of the car and strode purposefully to the unmarked car. "Who are you?" he demanded.

"Deputy sheriffs. Dade County."

"Let me see your identification."

"Let us see yours."

In the confusion and fumbling of wallets, Remo's snake quick hands darted through the steering wheel to the car keys, plucking them out too fast to jingle.

"Hey, what're you doing with the keys?"

"Nothing," said Remo as his thumb pressed the grooves and teeth of the ignition key out of line. "Just want to make sure you don't run anywhere until I see that identification."

The detectives at the wheel snatched back the keys. "You just watch your step there, fella. We're officers."

"All right. I'll let it go this time," said Remo in his best, decade-old patrolman's voice.

The two deputy sheriffs looked at each other in confusion. They were even more confused when Farger and the reporter who talked like a cop drove away, and their ignition key wouldn't work.

"The sonofabitch switched keys." But upon examination, that proved not to be the case. They tried the key again and it did not work again. Finally one of the deputies held the key to his right eye and sighted along the grooves. He noticed they were bent out of shape. As he tried to hammer the key back into shape with the butt of his revolver, Farger's car vanished over a hill.

Miles ahead, Remo noticed a lovely dirt road cutting into swamplands. Farger pulled in.

"You see what happened to the deputies?"

Remo shrugged. He pointed to a tree.

"Pretty wet over there," Farger said. "Do you think that's good?"

"Try it," said Remo.

So Willard Farger in his best Douglas MacArthur wading-ashore stride went to the tree and Remo drove the car right up to it into the wet mush.

"What're you doing? You crazy? That's my car," yelled Farger. He dove for the driver's seat. Remo snatched the ignition keys, slid out the passenger's door, and jammed it shut so it would not open. He pranced over the car top and down to the other side where he performed the same jamming operation on Farger's door.

"What're you doing, you crazy bastard?" screamed Farger.

"An interview."

"Open the damned door." Farger struggled with the handle, but it snapped off. The car sank into the dark ooze up to the midpoint of the hubcaps. Remo hopped to the dry spot of moss near the palm tree. He took a notebook out of his pocket and waited.

"Get me out of here," yelled Farger.

"In a minute, sir. First, I want your opinion on ecology, the urban crisis, the farm crisis, the energy crisis, the Indochina situation and the price of meat."

With a sudden belching sound, the front end of the car sank almost to the windshield. Farger climbed over the seat to the back. He hurriedly opened the window and tried to climb out headfirst. Remo left the dry spot to push Farger back inside.

"Let me out of here," yelled Farger. "I'll tell you anything."

"Where are the Bullingsworth papers?"

"I don't know. I never saw them."

"Who told you what to say, when you started shooting off your mouth about Folcroft?"

"Moskowitz. The city manager. He said Mayor Cartwright wanted me to do it."

"Did Moskowitz kill Bullingsworth?"

"No. Not that I know of. The Folcroft people did. Are you from Folcroft?"

"Don't be absurd," Remo said. "That organization doesn't exist."

"I didn't know that," cried Farger. "You gotta let me out of here." Muck oozed up into the car window and Farger raised the window just ahead of the slime.

"What was the point of you guys blabbing about the Folcroft thing?"

"It was Mayor Cartwright's idea. He said if we exposed it, they wouldn't be able to slap any of his men or him with phony, trumped-up indictments."

"I see. Thank you for the wonderful interview."

"You going to let me out of here?"

"As a newsman, I have a responsibility to report the facts, not interfere with them. Representing the Fourth Estate. . . ." Remo had no chance to finish the sentence because with a lurching slurp, Farger's car dropped and now only the roof of the sedan showed. Muffled moans came through it. Remo leaped to the roof. The car sank deeper from his weight and the swamp began to crowd his little platform.

As Chiun had taught him so long ago, Remo focused the power on his right hand and welding the fingers and palm into an almost straight line, slashed down into the thin metal roofing, creating a three-foot long scar. He ripped the thin topping off and Farger scrambled through the hole, his face red with sweat and tears.

"I just want you to know I'm not fooling around," Remo said. "Now take me to see Moskowitz."

"Sure, sure," Farger said. "I always considered the press my friend. You know, you conduct one hell of an interview."

When Remo and Farger hitched a ride into the city, Remo said he would reimburse Farger for the car.

"Don't worry about it," Farger said. "Insurance will cover it. You certainly do conduct one whale of an interview."

In the city Farger phoned Moskowitz. The city manager had just arrived home.

"One whale of a newsman wants to see you, Clyde," said Farger.

But the interview never took place. When Remo got to City Manager Clyde Moskowitz's house, the door was opened, the lights were on and Moskowitz was staring at a television set with a half-smile on his lips. His eyes were clouded. The lacquered wooden handle of an ice pick stuck out of his right ear. Remo stood near Moskowitz, looking at the ice pick, sensing the strange floral smell that it seemed to give off.

And then he felt very helpless. For the first time, Remo feared that the art of the assassin might not be enough.

CHAPTER EIGHT

"Marshal Dworshansky, your lilac cologne, sir." The valet offered the thin, silver bottle on the silver tray as the yacht lurched in the growing hurricane winds.

Marshal Dworshansky shook seven drops of the greenish cologne on his hand, and rubbed it between his open palms. Then he gently slapped his face and neck.

"Shall I have the cook select the meat, Marshal?"

Dworshansky shook his head. "No, Sasha, the important things a man must do himself. To my sadness, I have found out that to entrust others with a major task is to put your life in their hands."

"Very good, Marshal. The captain wishes to know when to return to port."

"Tell him to stay out here. Let us ride out the storm, Sasha, like seamen of old. How is my daughter taking the sea?"

"Like a true sailor, Marshal."

Dworshansky chuckled. "Ah. If she were a man, Sasha. If she were a man, she would show them a thing or two, eh, Sasha?"

"Yes, Marshal Dworshansky."

With two quick passes of a brush, Dworshansky formed his graying hair into a neat, presentable style—not quite a crew cut, but not flowing either. He dressed in white silk shirt and white cotton pants and white deck shoes. Neat, presentable and functional. He looked at himself in the mirror and slapped his hard stomach. He was in his sixties, yet still well-muscled and fat free.

When the captain signed on new, young, crew members, Dworshansky would offer them $100 if they could throw him in a wrestling match. When none achieved this, he would offer $200 if two men could do it as a team. That failing, he offered $300 for three and $400 for four. He would stop at four, never winded or even flushed with effort.

"Five of you might make me work up a sweat," he would say.

Now Dworshansky entered the ship's galley like a general on inspection. "The meat, Dmitri," he ordered. "It must be special tonight. Very special."

"Your daughter, Marshal?"

"Yes. And her daughter, my granddaughter."

"It is good to serve your entire family again, Marshal."

Dmitri, a short wide man with thick Slavic features and hands like soup bowls, hoisted a boar's carcass to the cutting block. With obvious pride, he waited for Marshal Dworshansky to inspect the provision. He was not disappointed.

"Dmitri, in a desert you could find ice water, and in Siberia, you could gather warm mushrooms, but in America you are even more magnificent. Where did you ever get a piece of real meat, hard meat without the heavy marbling of fat? Tell me how you did it, Dmitri. No. Don't tell me, for then your magic would be lost."

Dmitri dropped to one knee and kissed the marshal's hands.

"Up, up, Dmitri. None of that."

"I would die for you, Marshal."

"Don't you dare," said Marshal Dworshansky lifting the man to his feet. "And leave me to starve among these savages without my beloved Dmitri?"

"You will have boar in wine as none of your ancestores' ancestors has ever had," said Dmitri, and despite protestations, insisted upon kissing the marshal's hands again.

In the stateroom, Marshal Dworshansky saw his

daughter and granddaughter reading fashion magazines, the mother scarcely older-looking than her college-senior daughter, both with the fine high Dworshansky cheekbones, both with stunningly clear-blue eyes, and both the joy and the light of his life.

"Darlings," he called out, opening his arms. His granddaughter leaped into his arms as though she were still a toddler, laughing and showering kisses on his cheeks.

His daughter approached him with more mature steps, but the embrace was deeper and stronger, a mature woman's love for her father.

"Hello, papa," she said, and this would have surprised many people in Manhattan, who knew her as Dorothy Walker, president of Walker, Handleman and Daser, the queen of the cold bitches of Madison Avenue, the woman who had battled the giants and won.

One reason for Dorothy Walker's success was not, as many rumored, her ability to find the right bed at the right time, but her superior business sense, and another fact unknown to anyone outside this calm stateroom in a turbulent sea. Her little advertising agency was never little at all. It opened its doors with more than $25 million in assets, the personal dowry returned by her husband before he disappeared two decades before.

Unlike other little shops that begin with creative talents and hopes, Walker, Handleman and Daser began with the ability to go ten years without a client. Naturally, not needing business for survival, the agency found business ganging up at its front door.

"Have you been a good boy, papa?" asked Dorothy Walker, patting her father's flat stomach.

"I have not looked for trouble."

"I don't like the sound of that," said Dorothy Walker.

"Oh, grandpa. Are you doing exciting things again?"

"Teri is under the impression that your life has been a

romantic one, papa. I wish you had never told her those stories."

"Stories? They are all true, my dear."

"Which makes them worse, papa. Now, please."

"Oh, mommy. You're so out of it. Grandpa is so cool, so with it, and you keep putting him down. Really, mommy."

"Cool and with it, I can buy for $25,000 a year, take your choice of weight, size and hair styling. Your grandfather is too old and too mature to be out adventuring around the world."

"Enough controversy," said Marshal Dworshansky. "Tell me the good things that are happening to you."

Teri had a basketful of good things and she explained them in detail, each with a tense crisis and each of great import, from a new boyfriend to a professor who hated her.

"Which professor?" asked Marshal Dworshansky.

"Never mind, papa—and Teri, don't you tell him."

"Ah, my daughter is so fierce. Listen to your mother."

After the late dinner was over and after the granddaughter had gone to bed, Dorothy Walker, née Dworshansky, spoke seriously to her father.

"All right. What is it this time?"

"What is what?" asked the marshal with great innocence.

"Your happiness."

"I am happy to see my loved ones again."

"Papa, you can bullshit prime ministers and governors and generals and oil shieks. But you can't bullshit me. Now there is one happiness for seeing me and Teri, and another when you've been out in one of your street fights."

Marshal Dworshansky stiffened. "The Spanish Civil War was not a street fight. World War II was not a street fight. South America was not a street fight, nor was the Yemeni campaign."

"Papa, this is Dorothy you're talking to. I know, no matter how you plan things, you always wind up doing the dirty work yourself. And it makes you very happy. What is it this time? What is it that would make you break your promise to me?"

"I didn't break my promise. I did not seek this out. I was truthfully minding my own business," said Marshal Dworshansky, and then he told her about having cocktails with Mayor Cartwright in Miami Beach when he got some bad news. And all Marshal Dworshansky had said was a mere: "If I were in your shoes, I would not panic. I would. . . ."

And like so many other campaigns, this one had begun like that. A bit of good advice, then a promise of reward from those he served. Unlike other soldiers of fortune however, Marshal Dworshansky was not a penniless beggar who would settle for jewels or money. Like his daughter, he always went for bigger game. Not needing money, he demanded and got much more than money.

"I've never had a city before," he said. "And besides, the campaign is all over. Mayor Cartwright cannot lose."

"And how many ice picks have you left in how many ears?"

"Some things, as you know, are necessary to do, even when we do not take pleasure in them. But it should be over now. The enemy is stumped."

And when Marshal Dworshansky outlined who he thought the enemy was, his daughter looked away from him in anger.

"You know, papa, I used to resent those Polish jokes. But now, after hearing this, after listening to you so incredibly happy about your wonderful new enemy, I'm beginning to wonder if those jokes did not make us look a bit too intelligent."

Dworshansky was curious. He had never heard of a Polish joke.

"If you'd leave this yacht other than to cause mayhem or stick an ice pick in someone's ear, papa, you'd find out what the world is up to."

Intrigued, the marshal demanded to hear Polish jokes and to his daughter's reluctant good humor, he laughed uproariously at each.

"I've heard them before," he said, slapping a knee gleefully. "We used to call them Ukrainian jokes. Did you ever hear about the Ukrainian who went to college?"

Dorothy shook her head.

"Neither has anyone else," said Dworshansky and exploded in a booming laugh that reddened his face and brought him near helplessness everytime he repeated: "Neither has anyone else."

"That's a horrible joke, papa," laughed Dorothy Walker, not wanting to encourage her father, but his laughter was too contagious for her to resist.

For the rest of the night he told Ukranian jokes and would not stop even when his ship's radio operator interrupted to tell him Mayor Cartwright was trying desperately to reach him.

"An urgent problem, Marshal," said the radio operator. "Someone named Moskowitz is dead."

"Wladyslaw," said Marshal Dworshansky. "Have you ever heard about the Ukrainian who went to college?"

CHAPTER NINE

Hurricane warnings were sounded in the Miami Beach area, and a shaky Sheriff McAdow met with Mayor Cartwright in the mayor's spacious one-story ranchhouse, as dark winds whipped through palm trees on the lawn.

Cartwright turned away from his shortwave radio, his face flushed. He wore Bermuda shorts and a white tee shirt. An open bottle of bourbon sat on top of the set.

McAdow, ashen-faced, leaned forward.

"Nothing? Nothing?"

Cartwright shook his head.

McAdow, in white shirt with shining star and light gray pants with black leather holster, rose from his seat and went to the window. He shook his head.

"Your idea, Tim. Your idea."

Cartwright poured himself a half-tumbler of bourbon and downed it in two gulps. "Good. I confess. My idea. Sue me."

"Jesus, what did you get us into, Tim? What did you get us into?"

"Will you relax? Just relax. The marshal says we're in good shape."

"And he won't answer your radio message."

"He said we should sit tight and we're in good shape. Now damn it, until we hear from him or reach him, that's what we're going to do." Tim Cartwright filled the tumbler half-full again.

"We're in great shape. Great shape. Moskowitz is dead. Just like Bullingsworth got it. Farger is shitting in his pants because he says he met some guy who rips off car roofs, and we're sitting tight with orders to do nothing until further orders. Great shape. There's Farger out there carrying the ball, and he's as loose as lambshit, and Moskowitz is dead."

"I trust Dworshansky."

"So why are you drinking so heavy?"

"I'm celebrating early. My victory next week in my bid for reelection. 'Mayor Timothy Cartwright last night won an overwhelming victory in his re-election effort as he trouced one lunatic, 99 percent to one percent.' "

"You're so sure? Just because Dworshansky said so? Your great friend, military, political, organizational genius Dworshansky. The man countries bid for. Your friend."

"You agreed," Cartwright said.

"Everything happened so damned fast."

"Something else is damned fast," the mayor said. "You forgot damned fast that the feds were going to stick your ass in jail, and Dworshansky's maneuver has blown that all to hell."

"I'd rather do a stretch in jail than end up with an ice pick in my ear."

"We don't know if Dworshansky did it."

"And I don't know that he didn't."

"And if he did, so what? He told us, maybe some people had to die. I don't like it. You don't like it. But even worse, I don't like being poor and in jail."

Sheriff McAdow turned from the window. "I'll see you. I'm going back to headquarters. The lines will be buzzing like crazy in this weather."

"Go to it, Clyde. That's what you were elected for. Protect the people."

When the sheriff had left, Tim Cartwright filled his tumbler full and turned out the lights in the room. He watched the hurricane grow, the rain coming in torrents now, the city preparing to survive nature.

What had gone wrong? He hadn't run for office to be

on the take. He had run because he wanted to be somebody. He had come home from the second world war with the government owing him an education under the GI bill and a lot of thoughts about democracy and that way of government being the best for people to live under.

So how did he end up with a big fat bank account in Switzerland, scheming to stay out of jail? Even as a councilman, he wouldn't take. Sure, he needed campaign contributions and contractors who were helpful got a little extra consideration, but nothing out of the ordinary.

Was it the first time that the campaign treasury had a surplus, and he took the overage for himself? Or was it doing favors for nothing, and then wondering why he didn't do them for something?

Tim Cartwright could not place the first step toward actively seeking extraordinary profit from his office, but he knew the later ones. And they could send him to jail.

And so, not to go to jail, he entrusted his future to a man who claimed he knew how espionage worked. It had seemed very simple at first. Well, not really simple, but kind of daring-brilliant.

The fed spies had Cartwright and McAdow and Moskowitz. They knew the bank accounts and the graft and the shakedowns. So instead of trying to deny it and defend themselves, they were told: go on the attack. Make it impossible for the government to use its information.

And it had worked. An expendable piece of equipment, Willard Farger, had been sent off on a fool's errand—to attack the government—and it had worked. Cartwright was going to be re-elected next week, and the government would be afraid to move against him. And by the time the feds had gotten their wits back about them, well, Mayor Tim Cartwright might just have resigned his office and decided to go live out his twilight years in Switzerland.

"I promise you a long and happy life, free of jail," Marshal Dworshansky had said.

And there was only a small price. Give him the city. Whatever the Marshal wanted in greater Miami Beach, Cartwright had to provide. Cartwright hoped that Dworshansky would ask for the narcotics business. Cartwright had never wanted to be in on it, but the money was just too much to refuse.

Protect the people. Tim Cartwright downed the last of the tumbler and wanted to cry. He would have given anything at that moment not to have taken that little bit of campaign overage many years before.

In Folcroft Sanitarium, a Dr. Harold Smith appeared bewildered. Did the FBI men really believe someone with a Folcroft educational grant was doing some sort of political espionage?

Yes, was the answer.

Well, Dr. Smith's books and records were completely open to the FBI. Imagine someone doing something illegal with an educational grant. What was this world coming to?

"You're either naive or a genius," said an FBI agent.

"Neither, I'm afraid," Dr. Smith said. "Just an administrator."

"Just one question. Why are those windows one-way glass?"

"They were like that when the foundation purchased the estate," said Smith, who remembered how the dating on the billing had been changed more than a decade ago in preparation for just such an investigation. The whole organization had been set up to work just that way, from the computer tapes to the billing on the one-way glass.

The secret of CURE was holding. If it could hold just a little longer, Remo might be able to pull off the little miracle. Somehow, figure out a way to defuse the Miami Beach bomb that was blowing the cover off CURE. It was a slim chance, but it was CURE's only chance. Just wait. Wait for an all-clear from Remo.

In Miami Beach, nothing was clear. Hurricane Megan had seen to that. Even Chiun had been helpless, as his daytime serials were interrupted by static. The Master of Sinanju looked heavenward in anger and then to Remo's surprise, turned off the television.

"I've never seen you do that before, and in the middle of *As the Planet Revolves*."

"One cannot go against the forces of the universe. That is for fools. One should use those forces and thus become stronger."

"How can you use a hurricane?" asked Remo.

"If you need to know, you will know, when you are at peace with those forces."

"Well, I need to know, Little Father. I need to know something."

"Then you will know it."

"I will know it. I will know it," said Remo, imitating the high-pitched voice. "What will I know?" He went to a large oak table in the middle of the living room of the condominium apartment that he had leased in Chiun's name, using the last of the CURE money he had.

"What will I know?" he repeated and closed his right hand on the corner of the table. "To focus the forces of my mind," he said, snapping off the corner of the table as if it were thin plastic. "Hooray for the forces of the mind. We now have a broken table and I am still helpless.

"What will I know, Little Father? To keep the centrality of my balance?" And Remo's feet hit the wall, then went to the ceiling, as if yanked by wire cords, and then, back down to the carpet which he caught with his neck. He rolled erect to his feet. "Hooray for the forces of the mind. We now have footprints on the ceiling. Helpless. I'm as helpless as you are. We're helpless.

Don't you understand. We're just two crummy, helpless assassins."

"Just," said Chiun. "Just. Just. Just. You do not see. You do not hear and you do not think. Just. Just. Just."

"Just. Just helpless," and Remo repeated how he had started his mission to save CURE. He had gotten all that a frightened man could tell him.

Although Chiun was deeply offended, he nodded that this had been correct.

"And he gave me the name of another man."

Chiun nodded that this, too, was correct.

"But that man was dead."

Chiun nodded again, for there was still the alternative.

"So I waited for them to come after me."

Chiun nodded, for that, too, was correct. That was the alternative.

"And no one has come."

Chiun thought deeply and raised a long-nailed finger. "It is very difficult, my son, when your enemy will not help you. This is rare, I must admit, for most conflicts are won by those who help their foe the least. This I have taught you. Is there another person connected with this that you know?"

Remo shook his head. "Only one," he said. "The mayor. And if I should attack him, I would destroy myself, because it would mean that all his stories about CURE and Folcroft have been true. So I would gain nothing."

Chiun thought deeply again, and then he smiled.

"I have the answer. It is as simple as knowing who you are."

Remo was awed. The Master of Sinanju had seen through a difficult problem again.

"We have lost," Chiun said, "and knowing that, knowing that our current emperor has lost his kingdom, we will seek a new emperor, as Masters of Sinanju have done since there was a Sinanju and since there were emperors."

"That's your answer?"

"Of course," said Chiun. "You have said it yourself. We are assassins, not just assassins. Any man with a good mind can become a doctor, and being an emperor is an accident of birth, or, in your country, an accident of voters, and being an athlete is just the happenstance of body combined with effort, but to be an assassin, a Master of Sinanju, or a student of Sinanju—ah, that is something. That is not for everyone."

"You're as helpful as a hangover, Chiun."

"What is your problem? That you are what you are?"

Remo felt frustration mount to the border of rage. "Little Father. If the world were any sort of decent place to live, then I wouldn't be doing this . . . this."

"So that is it. You wish to change the world?"

"Yeah."

Chiun smiled. "Better to stop the hurricane with a string. Are you speaking truth to me?"

"Yes. That's what this organization that pays our salaries is about."

"I did not know that," said Chiun in amazement. "Changing the world. Then we are truly lucky that we leave this kingdom, for surely its emperor is mad."

"I'm not leaving. I'm not letting Smith down. You can leave if you wish."

Chiun waved a finger, signifying that he would not do this. "I have spent ten years transforming worthless, meat-eating self-indulgent flab into something almost approaching competence. I am not leaving my investment."

"All right, then," said Remo. "Do you have any usable suggestions?"

"For a man who wishes to change the world, no suggestion is usable. Unless of course you wish to stop the hurricane and transform it into little streams that feed the rice fields."

"How?" Remo said.

"If you cannot make your enemies fight your fight, then you must fight their fight, even if they should win. Because it is truly written that an unjust man finds success to be the greatest failure of all."

"Thanks," said Remo in disgust. He left the apartment and went downstairs, where the aged residents were discussing the hurricane and how hurricanes like this never happened in the Bronx, but Miami Beach was so much nicer, wasn't it?

Most of the people in the building were retired New Yorkers. Remo sat down in a sofa in the lobby to think. All right. He forced his mind clear. Farger had been a link, but he knew nothing. Moskowitz, the link after Farger, had been broken with an ice pick. Normal tactics called for Remo to go after Cartwright, but with Cartwright continually screaming that the government was out to get him, an attack by Remo would just lend weight to the charge, and CURE would be dead. Remo felt a finger poke his arm. It was a chubby old lady in a print dress with a warm smile. Remo tried to ignore her. The finger poked again.

"Yes," said Remo.

"You have such a lovely father," said the woman. "So sweet and gentle and kind. Not like my Morris. My husband Morris."

"That's nice," said Remo. How could he make his opponents fight?

"You don't look Korean," said the woman.

"I'm not," said Remo.

"I don't mean to be nosey, but how could that sweet loveable human being be your father if you're not Korean?"

"What?" said Remo.

"You're not Korean."

"No. Of course, I'm not Korean."

"You should be nicer to your father. He's too nice for words."

"He's a real sweetheart," said Remo sarcastically.

"I detect a tone of disapproval."

"He's wonderful. Wonderful," said Remo. Could Remo attack other officials in the city government? Ones not involved with the League papers? No. It would still be too close.

"You should listen to your father more. He knows best."

"Sure," said Remo. What could make the politicians come after him?

"Your father's given you so much. We all cried when we heard what you had done to him."

Remo suddenly tuned into the woman.

"I've done something to Chiun?" he asked. "You have spoken to Chiun?"

"Oh, everyone speaks to Chiun. He's so sweet. And to think his son won't carry on the tradition."

"Did he tell you what the tradition was?"

"Religious something or other we didn't understand. You help support starving babies or something. Overseas relief. Right? But you don't want to do that for a living, right? You should listen to your father. He's such a nice man."

"Please," Remo said. "I'm trying to think."

"You go ahead and think and don't let me bother you. I know you're not an ingrate like everyone in the building says."

"Thank you for your confidence," Remo said. "Please leave me alone."

"That's no way to talk to the only person in this building who doesn't think you're an ingrate."

Remo looked at his hands. They were useless.

"You should treasure your father. You should listen to him."

All right, lady. All right. I'll listen to Chiun. What did he say? If you can't make your opponents fight your fight, then fight their fight. What in the hell could that mean? Wait! Just suppose. Suppose Remo had a candidate for mayor, and he could elect him. They'd either have to come after Remo, or else lose the power they were fighting to keep. Of course, Because if Cartwright lost, he'd wind up in jail. Once you're in, you can always nail those who are recently out.

Okay. One for Chiun. But how? Could Remo lean on every voter? Absurd. What about a candidate? Anybody. But money? What about money? Remo no longer had access to CURE finances. All he had were his hands. His worthless hands.

For the first time in a decade, he had money troubles, a lot of them.

". . . . leaving that poor sweet old man alone upstairs what with all the robberies that have been taking place."

Remo tuned back in on the conversation. Beautiful. That was it. He rose from the sofa and kissed the startled woman on her cheek.

"Beautiful," he said. "Absolutely beautiful."

"Attractive, maybe," said the woman, "but beautiful, no. Now I have a granddaughter, she's beautiful. Are you married?"

CHAPTER TEN

The Dade County Airport was crowded and all flights to Puerto Rico were booked because of two days of weather delays.

Remo smiled at the reservations clerk who had said she would try to get him out on a flight the next day, and she said: "You're cute."

"So are you," Remo said. "We ought to check this thing out when I get back from Puerto Rico. But you've got to get me on the next flight."

"Let's check it out tonight," said the clerk in airlines blue. "You're not going to Puerto Rico tonight."

"Not even a standby?"

"Every flight tonight has at least a half dozen standbys. You'll never get off tonight."

"Put me on standby," said Remo. "I feel lucky."

"All right. But you'd be better off at my place. That's real lucky."

"You bet," said Remo, winking. Who knew if she voted in Miami Beach or not, and if he should be with his candidate, whoever he might be, and she saw him, she just might vote for that candidate. Now he knew why Chiun loathed politics. You had to be pleasant to people.

She gave him the flight number and Remo checked out the waiting area. It was packed. Good. He saw the doors to the loading platform where a uniformed clerk stood taking registrations and tickets. Good.

Remo spun around and went back down the aisle until he saw a waiting gate which was not in use. He ducked into it and went to a loading door which was locked. He cracked his way through it as if it were designed to be cracked by any passerby, and then was out into the rain-squawl remnant of the passed hurricane. Field lights blinked in the distance and he could see the colored lights over the control tower. How ironic, he thought. If CURE were still functioning, he would only have to phone Smith and he could get an Air Force plane if he wanted. And here he was trying to beat one of the peasants out of a seat on an economy special to San Juan.

He waited in the night rain getting soaked, until an operations attendant in white uniform with plastic ear protectors and baseball cap pulled over his head trotted toward one of the hangars.

Like a wind at midnight, Remo was out onto the slick asphalt and he took the man with a short slap at the back of the head, not enough for concussion but enough to put him out. The man hadn't even begun to crumple when Remo spun him around, back toward the gate door he had cracked through. Remo helped him out of his white coveralls, baseball cap and earphones. Remo rolled the man to where asphalt met siding and squeezed into the coveralls, pulling them on over his own suit jacket and pants. Then he put on the earphones and cap and was ready.

He moved along the side of the building counting doors until he got to his Puerto Rican flight. He was standing there when the doors to the airstrip opened.

"This flight 825 for Juan?" he yelled into the area.

A few passengers, waiting for him to get out of their way so they could go to the plane, mumbled yes. The ticket taker came from behind his counter and looked at Remo in the disdainful manner visited on people who work with their hands, by those in white shirts who make less.

"This is improper," said the clerk.

"Improper, hell. Is this flight taking off?"

"Of course it is."

Remo whistled low and shook his head.

"They never listen. They never listen. All right, let them save two thousand bucks a flight. Let them save it."

The clerk, a smooth-faced tedious compendium of propriety, raised his hands to shush Remo.

"Sure. Let everybody know but the passengers," Remo said.

"Will you shut up?" whispered the clerk angrily.

"Won't make no difference," Remo said loudly. "That jet hits five hundred feet, there ain't gonna be anybody around to complain. Pheew. Nobody."

"What's your name?" demanded the clerk.

"Just the guy who tried to save the lives of innocent people. We've had these engines in and out of the shop and we've been lucky. But in this weather, no luck is gonna carry this cheap outfit."

Remo turned to the passengers. A young mother cradled her child in her arms.

"Look," said Remo. "A little baby. For saving two grand on a crummy flight, a little baby. And his mother. You bastards."

With that, Remo pulled his head back in, slammed the door behind him and went back the way he came. He peeled off his coveralls and dropped them on the still sleeping figure of the airlines man.

When Remo returned to the ticket counter, he was pleasantly surprised. There was a sudden rash of cancellations for his flight.

"Lucky," Remo said.

"You sure are," said the girl. "I don't understand it."

"I live clean," said Remo squinching the rain from his hair.

A few people looked at him closely but none of the passengers on the "doomed" flight to San Juan recognized him as the flight attendant, whose emotional outburst had left the plane with a half dozen empty seats.

When the plane landed, Remo caught a cab to a large fish packer, a specialist in frozen fillets, who assured him that he packed for many major American brands.

But could the man ship on delivery? Was he reliable? "Absolutely, sir."

Remo wasn't sure. He was in the hotel business and he had to be sure of deliveries. If the man could guarantee him immediate air shipment, Remo might consider him for really large regular orders.

"In twelve hours, you can have any order you want."

Fine, Remo said. Tomorrow morning would be fine. He picked out the fish he wanted, and insisted the cartons be marked with an X painted red. Right now. On all fifty boxes. Now Remo wanted them shipped inside outer cartons with a good amount of dry ice.

"We know how to ship, señor."

Perhaps, but Remo knew what he wanted. He wanted red X's on the outside boxes also.

The packer shrugged. Remo gave the man the last of his money and said he would pay the rest in the morning.

"Cash?" asked the packer suspiciously.

"Of course," Remo said. "We're in a fast business. We only pay our regular suppliers by checks." Remo realized that made no sense at all, but he could tell that the packer thought there might be something slightly illegal about Remo's business, and the packer liked that. He liked it so much, he added a little charge to the shipment.

"For speedy delivery, señor."

Remo feigned mild outrage, the packer feigned mild innocence, and the deal was consummated.

When he left the packer, Remo had only enough money left for a cab to the new hotel strip just outside San Juan. For some strange reason, he felt suddenly hungry when he was unable to buy food. He had not wanted for anything since he was recruited.

Remo felt the hot sun of San Juan and let the hunger linger. That felt good, because he had been trained to control his hunger as he controlled his muscles and nerves. He enjoyed the pains in his stomach until they became unenjoyable and then, as he had been taught years before by the Master of Sinanju, he brought relaxation down his chest and into his stomach.

The Japanese Samurai, Chium had said, pretended they had eaten a meal and in this way tricked their minds into tricking their stomachs. This was a bad way to deal with hunger because it was an untruth, and he who loses the truth with himself becomes blind in a small way, and to be blind was to die.

In Sinanju, the masters knew their bodies and would not tell them lies. Hunger was the body telling the truth. Do not deny the pain, but accept it and leave it. You will have the pain, but not as something that bothers you.

Remo had thought he would never understand and never learn, but his body learned without him, and one day he was just doing the things Chiun had taught him, although he did not know how he did them.

Remo located the power station he wanted, and waited then until the darkness of past midnight. He checked the very light plastic suit folded into his jacket pocket and the rubber mask folded in the other. No point in going ahead unprepared, he thought.

Inside the power station, Remo eloquently explained to the chief engineer what he wanted.

"Show me how to turn off the power for several hours or I'll break your other arm."

The chief engineer, rolling on the floor in agony, thought this offer made eminent sense. He mumbled something Remo could hardly understand about backing up and currents and all the things chief engineers were expected to know about. What it came down to was pulling the lever on the top of the panel and the lever on the bottom at the same time.

"The one with the little squidget kind of thing?" asked Remo.

"*Si,*" said the engineer, moaning.

"Thanks," said Remo, and pulled both levers simultaneously. He was in darkness. San Juan's hotel strip, across the highway from him, was in darkness too.

"I will wait here and if you so much as move," Remo said, "I will kill you." And then, with the quiet of a lynx on a fur blanket, Remo was out of the power station with the engineer still believing that the monster was with him.

The El Diablo and the Columbia Hotels are the largest on the strip, separated only by an alley. Their gambling rooms stay open until 4 a.m., but now in the predawn darkness, the gambling stopped, and men reached for candles and flashlights. Remo was into the El Diablo by the front door as bellboys and managers searched for lights. The night manager of the hotel knew exactly what to do in a power blackout. When the lights went out, he slammed shut the safe, according to regulatory precautions.

He stood by it with a pistol, according to regulatory precautions.

What was not in the regulations was the incredibly severe pain at the base of his spinal column. He was told how he could end the pain and since he wanted that more than anything else in the world, he did what he was told. He opened the safe by the light of a candle, and when it was opened, and Remo saw where the bundles and bags of gambling money were, he blew out the candle. From his jacket pocket, he removed the full rubber head mask and stuffed the face with money. He filled the chest cavity of the suit with money, and moving his arm into the empty arm of the one-piece jumpsuit, held the chest money which supported the head money, and for all practical purposes, it looked as if he held a dummy at the end of his arm.

Except in the darkness, it did not look like a dummy, but a man who was holding on to Remo for support. Remo moved through the bustling confusion and vagrant flashing lights, saying "Man injured. Man injured."

But no one could be bothered with an injured man. After all, was that not the night manager yelling about a robbery?

"Injured man," yelled Remo as he crossed the alley to the Columbia Hotel, but he was ignored, for men's jobs were at stake and these jobs depended on the most important thing at a casino. Money.

"Injured man," yelled Remo, moving to the manager's office of the Columbia.

"Get that sonofabitch out of here," yelled the manager of the Columbia, thinking that if there ever was a negligence suit, he could deny what he had said in court, and it would be his word against the word of the two guests.

Then he no longer cared about his word or anyone else's word. He cared only about the incredible pain in his stomach. He too was told how he could make the pain stop, and he did, so Remo put him to sleep and filled out the rest of the dummy suit with more money.

Into the lobby went Remo, only now, for the police, he was a drunk with a drunken buddy, trying to tell them how to do their job.

"You get the hell out of here," ordered a police captain, "or you're under arrest."

Chastened the two drunks moved off, out of the lobby, into the night. Remo felt a hand on his shoulder and turned to see a policeman, high-peaked island hat and all.

"Okay, buddy," the cop said, "I know your game.

Something big is happening, and you want to get arrested, so that later you can brag about how you were arrested on the big night. Well, we're not stupid mainland gringos here. So get moving."

And roughly, the police officer pushed Remo and his friend past the squad cars, down the street, and the officer waited until the two drunks had left.

"Damned gringo and their emotional problems," said the officer, who had just taken a course in psychology for a promotion he hoped someday to get.

The packing house was closed when Remo broke a window lock, made his way to the freezer, found the boxes marked with the red X, and replaced much of the dry ice with money. He kept two handfuls of one hundred dollar bills, and then left through the window. He shredded the suit and mask in a nearby trash can and waited for the manager to arrive.

"Punctual," Remo said, as the manager arrived with the first rays of dawn. "I like that." Remo paid the remainder of the charges in cash and promised an order five times as big if this delivery was really as prompt as the manager promised. He made this promise as sincerely as possible, because he was entering politics and one had to be sincere in politics when one told lies.

The manager personally drove his new customer to the airport. On the trip, Remo mentioned several names he had read in a CURE report, men whose Mafia connections Stateside were immaculate. The manager caught the drift of the conversation and assured Remo of his fidelity.

"Fidelity is a very healthy thing," said Remo.

The manager understood completely.

Remo gave him a little present for himself. A half-inch of money.

"You are too generous," said the manager, wondering exactly what Remo's mob connections were.

"Spend it in good health," Remo said. "Be sure to spend it in good health."

On the plane, Remo read in the San Juan paper the reports of the robbery. Brilliant, cunning, masterfully executed, well planned. The paper reported that a team of men—one injured—simultaneously robbed the two largest hotels. The cash loss was estimated at $2.5 million.

Remo would have to check that out against his fish which were due to arrive in Miami an hour after he did. He didn't think he had gotten that much. Probably employees had filched some. Maybe even the police. These things happened sometimes during big robberies. He felt angry that there were so many crooks in the world.

He went to the *New York Times,* feeling self-righteous and self-satisfied. Nothing there about the robbery. It had happened too late for the early edition of the Times which was flown to the island.

In the back sections of the paper was a picture of a stunning, knockout blonde in an evening gown. She was, the caption said, the Madison Avenue genius, Dorothy Walker of Walker, Handleman and Daser. An accompanying story said that her firm had never lost an account, and never failed to sell the client's product. Remo looked at the face that stared at him off the page. Smart, cultured, professional, and she looked as if she had great boobs, to boot.

Done. Decided. Walker, Handleman and Daser, which had never lost, would run the campaign for Remo's candidate for mayor. All he needed was a candidate for mayor, and that would be no problem for a man who was, as the San Juan robbery reports had it, "brilliant, cunning, a masterful planner."

"Brilliant," he mumbled to himself, reading again about the robbery. Perhaps if he had been running CURE instead of Smith, there never would have been the foulup and the leak in Miami Beach. Well, he would plug up the leaks and get Smith out of his little jam, try to give him some advice on proper security.

Chiun was wrong when he advised Remo to know what he could do and what he could not do. He was wrong in limiting his vision to doing what his father had done before him. That was the Oriental mind. Remo was American. There were new horizons, especially for brilliant and cunning people. How Chiun was afraid for people who thought they were brilliant.

"When you think you are brilliant, my son," he had said, "that is the beginning of stupidity, for you shut out all those senses that tell you of your weaknesses. And he who does not know his weaknesses cannot feed the babies of Sinanju."

CHAPTER ELEVEN

Hurricane Megan had passed and Miami Beach basked again in tropical mellowness. The Master of Sinanju sat on his balcony, warming himself in the dying sun, contemplating the disaster of someone with skills, Sinanju skills, lowering himself to politics. It was not a pleasant contemplation.

In his life, he had had two pupils. One, although Korean, a relative, and a villager of Sinanju, had been a complete loss. The other had proved to be a pleasant surprise, a white man, an American white man who had learned with exceeding swiftness the teachings of Sinanju.

And Chiun had taught him thus. He had taken a white man and made him almost worthy to assume the role of Master of Sinanju. With a Japanese, it would have been almost impossible, but with a white man, it was unthinkable, yet Chiun had done this thing, teaching his pupil to know the forces of man and nature, and to assume the responsibility for feeding Sinanju when the time came for its current master to return his body to the waters of time.

Now this pupil was to become a salesman of people. The thought made Chiun very unhappy. It was as if a beautiful swan were to try to burrow through the mud like a worm. He would have to tell Remo that, but Remo still had a way of not listening.

The doorbell buzzer interrupted the thoughts of the Master of Sinanju and he left his balcony to answer it. It was Mrs. Ethel Hirshberg with her friends. They had come to keep him company.

Chiun liked these women, especially Mrs. Hirshberg,

who had come to his rescue at the baggage rack at the airport. They knew how to understand tragedy and mourning. That appreciated what it was like to have children who did not appreciate what their parents had done for them. They appreciated the great daytime television dramas, the finest art form of the western world. And they played Mah Jongg.

That the woman did not know they were in the presence of the deadliest single killer in the world was not due to a lack of perception. People only understand what they already know, and seeing this frail old man with such sensitive features, hearing him talk of the babies of Sinanju, they naturally believed he raised money for babies, because they, in their lives, had spent much time raising money for such causes. They did not know that the babies of Sinanju were fed by deaths, performed for salary by the Master.

Such was their concern and affection for Chiun that when a mugger was reported in the building the night before, they all ran out with pots and pans to save Chiun, because they knew he was taking his evening stroll at the time. Fortunately, the mugger was found in a stairwell. Police theorized that he had been hit with a sledgehammer in the chest, although no sledgehammer was found and although the coroner privately pointed out that to inflict so much damage, the sledgehammer would have had to be dropped from a height of four miles. But the coroner said nothing publicly, since a mugger was a mugger was a mugger, and however they were gotten rid of was a benefit to mankind, in his opinion.

In the opinion of the ladies of the apartment building, it was goodness coming to goodness that Chiun had been spared.

Now they had a surprise for him. One of the ladies' sons was a writer for the most successful adventure show of the season. And wouldn't Chiun be happy to know it was about an Oriental?

"It's coming on now," squealed Mrs. Hirshberg.

Chiun sat on the large sofa between Mrs. Hirshberg and Mrs. Levy He watched the opening credits tolerantly, as the hero of the series trudged across the desert sand. But he moved forward on the couch to watch an opening flashback when the hero relived his childhood in the Orient and his training in the arts of combat.

He sat that way, shaking his head, through the entire show, and as soon as it was over, he bade the women good night because he was tired.

He still sat on the sofa whenRemo came home.

"There was a very evil thing on the television tonight," he said as Remo came through the door.

"Oh?"

"Yes, an evil thing."

"Oh. Am I allowed to know what this evil thing was?"

"A program told of the Shaolin priests, as if they were wise and good men " Chiun said this in a voice that reached for outrage, then looked to Remo as if for solace.

"So?" Remo said.

"The Shaolin were chicken thieves, who took refuge from the police in a monastery. And because it was better to have them in a monastery than in the countryside stealing chickens, they were allowed to live there and to masquerade as priests."

"I see," Remo said, although he did not see at all.

"You do not see at all," Chiun said. "It is evil to deceive people into believing well of people of whom only ill should be thought."

"It's only a show, for crying out loud," Remo said.

"But think of the people it can mislead."

"Well, then, write a letter to the producer and complain."

"Do you think that will do any good?"

"No," Remo said, "but it'll make you feel better."

"Then I will not do that. I will do something else."

Remo showered. When he came out, Chiun was seated at the table in the kitchen, pencil in hand, paper in front of him.

He looked up at Remo.

"How do you spell Howard Cosell?" he asked.

CHAPTER TWELVE

Of course, Willard Farger remembered Remo. How could he ever forget such a good interviewer? No, no, no, he wasn't nervous; he always sweated in the spring heat of Dade County. Certainly. Even in his air-conditioned home.

"That's good," Remo said. "A little sweat is good for a man who's going to be the next mayor of Miami Beach."

Farger looked at Remo closely to see if he were joking, then thought it over for a full tenth of a second and smiled because the thought gave him pleasure, then shook his head in resigned sadness. "Maybe someday, but not this year."

"Why not?" Remo said.

"It's too late. The election's next week. There's no way to get on the ballot this year."

"No way?"

"No way," Farger said. "I made my move too late." He was beginning to relax just a little, as each passing second made his assurance grow that Remo was not, for the moment, going to bury him in a swamp or bury an ice pick in his head.

"Could you replace a candidate if one, say, dies?" Remo asked coldly, and Farger stopped relaxing. He sat up straight in his chair.

"No. I'm the fourth deputy assistant commissioner of elections. I know the law. There's no way."

Remo leaned back on Farger's living room couch and propped his feet up on a plastic tile coffee table.

"Okay, then. If you can't be mayor, you'll make a great campaign manager. Who do we support?"

Farger took a deep breath. Without even thinking, he started off, "That's where I draw the line, Mr. Remo. I have supported Mayor Cartwright since he first sought public office; I have no intention now of deserting his leadership, doubly so since it is now under attack by an insidious encroachment of the federal. . . ."

"Do you want to join your car?" Remo interrupted.

Farger shook his head.

"All right. Then you're the campaign manager. Now who is our candidate? Besides Cartwright."

"But . . . I'll lose my job."

"There are worse things to lose."

"And my pension rights."

"You have to live to spend it."

"And my family. How will they live?"

"How much do you make a year?" Remo asked.

"Ten-five," Farger said.

Remo reached inside his jacket pocket and pulled out two sheaves of bills. He tossed them on the coffee table. "There's two years pay. Now who do we support?"

Farger looked at the money, at Remo, then at the money again, as his brain made calculations behind his narrowed eyes. "You can't support Cartwright?"

"No," Remo said. "Anyone who'd lie about the federal government the way he did . . . who'd deceive an honest, decent man like you into lying, can't be returned to office. Who else is running?"

"That's the problem," Farger said. "Nobody's running."

"Come on," Remo said. "What is Cartwright, a king or something? Of course, someone else is running."

"Well, there are some people," said Farger, with an inflection of distaste that, if recorded, would have ended forever his dreams of the presidency.

"Who are?"

"One is Mrs. Ertle McBargle. She's head of 'Abortion Now.' Then there's Gladys Tweedy. She's with the SPCA and wants to turn the town into an animal compound."

"Forget them," Remo interrupted. "No women."

Farger shrugged and sighed. "And then there's Mac Polaney."

"Yeah?"

"This is the 47th time he's run for public office. The last time he ran for President. When he didn't win, he said the country wasn't ready for him. He's not wrapped too tight."

"What does he do?"

"A disabled veteran. Lives on a pension. He lives on a houseboat down along the bay."

"How old?"

Farger shrugged. "Fiftyish?"

"Honest?"

"So honest he makes people sick. When he came back from service, everybody was trying to do something for veterans, so somebody got the bright idea to give him a job with the county. Fanfare, newspaper publicity and all."

"What happened?"

"He quit the job three weeks later. He said that nobody gave him any work to do. If I remember right, he said that wasn't unusual because no one seemed to know anything about work, most of all their own. And in like vein."

"Sounds like our man," Remo said. "An honest, decorated war hero with vast political experience."

"A poetry-spouting ninny who won't get a thousand votes."

"How many will vote next week?"

"Forty thousand or so."

"Then all we got to do is get 20,000 more for . . . what's his name?"

"Mac Polaney."

"Yeah. Mac Polaney, Mayor Polaney. Mayor Mac Polaney. The people's choice."

"The world's choice . . . nitwit."

"That's no way for his campaign manager to talk," Remo reminded Farger. "Now what are his special issues? What horses are we going to ride to victory at the polls?" He had heard a campaign manager once who sounded just like that.

Farger allowed himself a sneak's smile. "Just a minute," he said. "See for yourself. I've got it right here." He handed Remo a copy of the Miami Beach Journal, already turned to an inside page.

Remo took it and read:

CANDIDATE CALLS FOR BLACKOUT
OF POLITICAL CAMPAIGN ACTIVITY

It was a little headline, accompanied by a little story which read:

Mac Polaney, making his 48th try for public office in next week's mayoral race, today called upon all the other mayoral candidates to join him in halting all campaign activity.

"The weather has turned nice," Polaney said, in what he said would be his campaign's only press release, "and it's a great time to go fishing. So I'd like to invite the other candidates to join me on my houseboat for a fishing trip through the bay. That way, without politicians yakking around the city, people can enjoy the nice weather. (The lady candidates can bring chaperones; Mayor Cartwright can bring his keeper.)

"Sunshine is nicer than politicians anyway and fishing is great for the soul. So what do you say, man and ladies, let's cast our lines into God's great blue waters."

"The other candidates declined to comment."

Remo put the newspaper back onto the table. "The

perfect man for us," he said. "The first politician I ever heard who had his finger on the people's pulse."

"Now wait," Farger said. "That's not all. Last week, he called for the abolition of the police department. He said that if everybody would just promise not to commit any more crimes, we wouldn't need police. And then we could cut taxes."

"Good idea," Remo said.

"And before that," Farger said in growing desperation, "he said we ought to abolish the street-cleaning department. If he was elected mayor, he said, he would assign a different city councilman each day to duty picking up candy wrappers."

"Obviously an activist," Remo said. "Willing to dig in and face up honestly to the problems confronting us."

"No," Farger shouted, startling himself by his loudness. Softly, he said, "No, no, no, no, no. If I get involved with him, my political career is dead."

"And if you don't, Willard, you're dead. Now make up your mind."

There was a millisecond pause in the living room before Farger said:

"We'll need a campaign headquarters."

CHAPTER THIRTEEN

Mac Polaney's houseboat was tied up to an old tire, nailed to a rickety dock on a small rivulet that muddied its way inland from the bay.

The next mayor of Miami Beach was wearing green flowered shorts, a red mesh undershirt, black sneakers with no socks and a chartreuse baseball cap. He sat on a folding lawn chair on the deck of the houseboat, stringing gut leader onto fishhooks, when Remo drove up, got out of his car and walked to the boat.

"Mr. Polaney?" Remo said.

"Won't do you no good, son," Polaney said without looking up. He was, Remo gauged, in his early fifties, but he had the strong, melodic voice of a younger man.

"What won't do me any good?"

"I won't name you secretary of defense. No how, no how. I don't even think Miami Beach needs a secretary of defense. Maybe Los Angeles. I mean, anybody who knows Los Angeles knows that they could start a war. But not Miami Beach. Nope. So you ain't got a chance, son. Might just as well move along."

As if to accentuate the point, his shoulders hunched forward and he bent to his work of hook-rigging with increased fervor.

"But how are we going to deal with the Cuban missile threat?" Remo said. "Only ninety miles away, aimed right down our gullets."

"See. That's what I mean," Polaney said, standing up and looking at Remo for the first time. He was a tall lean man, tanned to a nut brown, with laugh wrinkles around the eyes that threatened to squeeze them shut.

"You militarists are all alike. One bomb, two bombs, four bombs, eight bombs . . . where does it end?"

"Sixteen bombs?" Remo suggested.

"Sixteen bombs, thirty-two bombs, sixty-four bombs, one hundred and twenty-eight bombs, two hundred and fifty-six bombs, five hundred and twelve bombs . . . what's after five hundred and twelve?"

"Five hundred and thirteen?"

Polaney chuckled. His eyes did shut. Then he snapped them open wide. "Pretty good," he said. "How would you like to be city treasurer?"

"Well, I had my heart set on being secretary of defense. But I'll take it. As long as I don't have to do anything dishonest."

"I'd never ask you to," Polaney said. "Just vote for me. And smile once in a while. Mark my words bub, the Cuban missile threat will take care of itself if we just give it a chance. Most threats and crises do. The only thing you can really do to screw them up is to try to solve them. If you just let things alone, they'll work out."

"You hand out job offers pretty freely," Remo said.

"You bet your sweet everloving. You're the three hundred and seventy first person I've offered the treasury to." He pulled a pad out from under a Coca Cola crate on the deck. "What's your name? Gotta write it down."

"The name's Remo. But how can you do that? Promise everybody the same job?"

"Easy, bub. I ain't gonna win."

"That doesn't sound like a politician talking."

"Politician? Me? Heck. All I know about politics is that I can't win."

"Why not?"

"First of all, I don't have any support. No one's gonna vote for no old fisherman. Second, I don't have any money. Third, I can't get any money because I won't make any deals with the people who've got money. So I lose. Q.E.D."

"Why do you keep running?"

"I think it's a man's duty to contribute to the governmental process."

"Most people do it by voting," Remo said.

"That's true, bub. But I don't vote. At least not in the city. Not for any of those crooks that run. So, if I can't vote, I've got to do something else. So I run. And lose."

Remo, overwhelmed by the sheer majesty of the logic, paused momentarily before asking: "How'd you like to win?"

"Who would I have to kill?"

"Nobody," said Remo. "That's my department. All you'd have to do is be honest. Don't go on the take. Don't go shaking down contractors. Don't make deals with the mob."

"Hell, son, that's easy. All my life, I've been not doing those things."

"Then you just have to keep doing what comes naturally. You interested?"

Polaney sat back down on the lawn chair. "You'd better come aboard and tell me what's on your mind."

Remo hopped up onto the deck railing, and then lightly skipped over it. He sat on the Coke case next to Polaney.

"Just this," he said. "I think you can win. I'll put up the money. I'll get your campaign managers, your workers. I'll handle the advertising and the commercials."

"And what do I do?" Polaney asked.

"Do what you want. Fish a little. Maybe if you feel like it, campaign a little." Remo considered that for a moment, then quickly added, "Better yet. We'll get pros in. See what they say about whether you should campaign or not."

"All right, bub. Your moment for truth telling. What do you get out of it?"

"The knowledge that I've helped to clean up a great city by putting an honest man in the mayor's office."

"That's all?"

"That's all."

"No sewer contracts?"

Remo shook his head.

"You don't want to build schools with watered-down cement?"

Remo shook his head.

"You don't want to name the next police commissioner?"

"Not even the next city treasurer," Remo said.

"Those are all the right answers, boy. Cause if you said yes to any of them, you were like to go for an unscheduled swim in the river."

"I don't swim," Remo said.

"And I don't play ball."

"Good. Then we understand each other."

Polaney put down the hooks he held in his gnarled leathered hands and fixed Remo with his pale blue eyes. "If you got all this money you say you got, how come Cartwright let you get away? He watches out for rich fish like you."

"I couldn't support Cartwright," Remo said. "Not after all this nonsense about League papers and stuff. Not after those cheap attacks on the federal government."

Polaney's eyes narrowed as he looked at Remo, then wiped his forehead with the back of his wrist. "You don't look like a nut," he said.

"I'm not. Just somebody who loves America."

Polaney sprang to his feet and slapped his hat over his heart in a civilian salute. Then Remo saw the small nickel-and-dime store flag on the rear of the boat. He wondered if he should chance a laugh. Polaney reached down a strong hand and yanked Remo to his feet. "Salute, boy. It's good for the soul."

Remo put his hand over his heart and stood there,

side by side with Polaney. Here we are, he thought, the two biggest lunatics in the Western Hemisphere. One lunatic wants to be mayor, and the other lunatic wants to make the first lunatic get his wish.

Finally, Polaney clapped his hand to his side, before putting his hat back on.

"I put my life in your hands," Polaney said. "What do you want me to do?"

"Go fishing," Remo said. "See if you can come up with anything not too greasy. I can't eat oily fish. And I'll be in touch."

"Son," Polaney said. "You're a flake."

"Yeah. Ain't it the truth. Now let's go win an election. And don't forget. No oily fish."

"How about that for a campaign slogan?"

"I don't think it's got enough crowd appeal," Remo said. "Anyway, I've got an idea for an advertising agency. Let them pick a slogan."

He hopped down to the dock and headed back for his car. Halfway there, he turned. "Hey, Mac," he called. "What made you think I wanted to be secretary of defense?"

Polaney was already back at work on his hooks. Without looking up, he said: "I saw you get out of the car. You look like a man who might start a war." He turned to Remo. "Right?"

"I'd rather finish one," Remo said.

CHAPTER FOURTEEN

"Walker, Handleman and Daser."

"Who's in charge there?" Remo asked the telephone voice.

"What does it have reference to?" the female voice answered, over the 1,500 miles of distance between Florida and New York.

"It has reference to $100,000 for a week's work," Remo said, hoping the girl was impressed.

"Just a moment, sir." She was.

So was Mr. Handleman to whom Remo talked next. Equally impressed was Mr. Daser to whom Remo talked after that. They were so impressed they were going to try to reach Dorothy.

"Dorothy?"

"Yes. The Walker of Walker, Handleman and Daser."

Remo nodded to himself, remembering the blonde of the *New York Times*. "Just walk over to her office and tell her you've got a fish on a line."

"I'm sorry, Mr. . . . er . . . you didn't give your name."

"That's right, I didn't give my name."

"She's on vacation."

"Where?" Remo asked.

"She's visiting her father in Miami Beach."

"That's where I am," Remo said. "Where can I reach her?"

"I'll have her call you," Mr. Daser said.

"Try to do it fast," Remo said and gave Daser the number where he could be reached. "The name is Remo," he said.

Ten minutes later the telephone rang again.

"This is Dorothy Walker," a cultured Manhattan voice said.

"I'd like you to run a campaign for me."

"Oh? What kind of campaign?"

"A political campaign."

"I'm sorry. We don't do political campaigns."

"Look. I'm talking about $100,000 for a week's work."

"Mr. Remo, I'd like to help, but we don't do political campaigns."

"You can sell air conditioners that don't work and paper towels with the absorbency of sandpaper and cigarettes that are made out of sawdust and you can't elect a mayor for Miami Beach?"

There was a pause. Then, "I didn't say we couldn't, Mr. Remo. I said, we don't. Who is your candidate by the way?"

"A gentleman named Mac Polaney," Remo said. Thinking of the gaunt fisherman on his homemade houseboat, Remo said: "A courtly, cultured gentleman. A decorated veteran of World War II, with a reputation for honesty, broad political experience. A PR man's dream."

"You make it sound very inviting, Mr. Remo. Let me call you back. But don't get your hopes up. We don't handle political campaigns."

"You'll handle this one," said Remo, confidently, "particularly if you meet our candidate. To meet him is to love him."

"And he's a politician?"

"Yes."

"Sounds unbelievable."

"He's an unbelievable man," Remo said.

"I'm beginning to think so are you. You've almost made me interested."

"Call me back soon," Remo said.

Remo hung up and sprawled out on his couch to await the return call. Less than two miles away, Dorothy Walker hung up the telephone, left her luxurious cabin and walked to the bow of the ship where her father, Marshal Dworshansky, sat in the sun.

He was very interested in her caller, as she had known he would be. "He offered you one hundred thousand dollars?"

"Yes. But I stalled him."

Marshal Palansky clapped his hands in glee. "Take it," he said. "This is the man we've been waiting for, and now he is delivering himself right into our hands. Marvelous," he chortled. "Marvelous. Take it."

"But how will I handle it?" his daughter said. "One week to do a political campaign?"

"My dear, I know you believe in the power of advertising and public opinion. However, in this case, the only opinion that counts is mine. The campaign is over. Nothing can stop Mayor Cartwright from winning. So do whatever you want for this Mr. Remo."

"Why bother if he's no threat?"

"Because he is the enemy, and it is good to know what the enemy plans."

Minutes later, Dorothy Walker was back in her stateroom calling Remo.

"We've decided. . . .," she began.

"We?"

"I've decided it's about time that Walker, Handleman and Daser moved into politics. This will be a great campaign in which to practice our new theories of communication. The idea of maximum message carrying to maximum quanta of people at. . . ."

"At maximum cost," Remo interrupted. "Look, you and I have gotten along fine by talking English. Let's continue that way, all right? You just do whatever it is you people do, and don't tell me about it."

"As you wish," Dorothy Walker said, and then, because she was interested in her father's enemy, she added: "Perhaps we could discuss the financial arrangements tonight. At dinner?"

"Okay," Remo said. "Pick someplace where you have credit. You're supposed to wine and dine us wealthy eccentric clients, aren't you?"

"De rigeur," she said.

Remo had had enough experience with newspaper photos not to expect too much of Dorothy Walker in person. He would not have been shocked if she had shown up looking like Maria Ouspenskaya, fresh off a gypsy wagon.

But he was not prepared for what showed up at the Ritz Hotel, where he waited in the massive dining room, sipping water.

First came Dorothy Walker, stunningly blonde and tan, a fortyish beauty who looked twenty. And with her was a twenty-year-old blonde carbon copy who seemed to have the look of having tantalized men for forty years. They wore matching aqua cocktail dresses.

A sound meter could have charted their progress along the aisle of the dining room, because each table stilled in succession as they walked by, following the *maître d'*, whose show of attention let it be known that they were very important people indeed.

"Mister Remo?" the older woman asked when she arrived at his table.

Remo stood up. "Miss Walker?"

"Mrs. Walker. And this is my daughter, Teri."

The waiter seated them, and Dorothy Walker said, "Well, what do you want us to do for all that money?"

"If I told you, you'd have me arrested."

"One never knows," she laughed. "One never knows."

They ate baked stuffed clams, sizzling in melted butter, and while Remo toyed with a piece of celery, he and Mrs. Walker reached agreement on the deal. One hundred thousand dollars for one week's work, with

Remo to pay all additional costs, including newspaper space, air time, and production costs.

"Should I have my lawyer draw a contract?" Mrs. Walker asked.

"I deal in handshakes," Remo said. "I trust you."

"I trust you too, but even though we've never done political campaigns, I know something about them," Dorothy Walker said. "All payment must be in advance because, God forbid, a candidate should lose—they never pay."

"That's called incentive to make sure your candidates never lose," Remo said. He moved a hand toward his inside jacket pocket. "You want the money now?"

"No hurry. Tomorrow will be fine."

The women ate escarole salad with Roquefort dressing, as Remo munched on a radish.

"Teri will handle the campaign for you," Dorothy Walker said. "Because of my position, I can't take it publicly. But having Teri means that you'll have me." Her eyes smiled at Remo. He wondered if she had meant anything more than business by that sentence. "You understand?"

"Of course," Remo said. "You want to be able to take credit if we win, but you don't want to be tagged personally with a loser."

Mrs. Walker laughed. "That's right. By the way, I've checked around. There is no way your Mr. Mac Polaney can win. He is regarded as the quintessential nut in a town of quintessential nuts."

"There are more things happening in heaven and earth than are dreamed of on Madison Avenue," Remo said.

The women had veal *cordon bleu* and Remo had rice, which Mrs. Walker pretended not to notice but which Teri Walker found exciting.

"Why just rice?" she said.

"Zen," Remo said.

"Wow."

"We want total artistic control," Dorothy Walker said. "We won't work any other way."

"That means you decide on commercials and advertising and slogans?" Remo asked.

She nodded.

"Well, of course," Remo said. "Why would I hire you if I wanted to do things myself?"

"You'd be surprised at how many clients don't feel that way," Dorothy Walker said.

During coffee, Mrs. Walker excused herself for the ladies' room.

Remo watched Teri Walker closely as she drank her coffee, her fine, tanned young muscles moving sleekly as she moved slightly in her chair.

She bubbled at him with conversation about his goals for urban government, the nature of Mac Polaney, and about something which she called "the handle we have to get on this campaign."

"Your first campaign?" Remo asked.

She nodded.

"Mine too," he said. "We'll learn together."

She finished the last sip of her coffee and asked Remo, "By the way, why'd you pick us?"

"Somebody told me you and your mother had great boobs. I figured I might as well enjoy looking at the campaign staff."

Teri Walker laughed, loud and full throated.

"Grandpa will just love you," she said.

Willard Farger had rented a suite of six connecting rooms in the Maya Motel. He called it campaign headquarters and staffed it with three girls who looked as if they had last campaigned in a Las Vegas chorus line.

"They're secretaries," Farger insisted to Remo. "Somebody's got to type and answer phones and things."

"I see," Remo said. "Where are the phones and typewriters and things?"

Farger snapped his fingers. "I knew there was something I forgot."

Remo beckoned Farger with a crooked finger and led him into one of the back rooms. He locked the door behind them. "Sit down," he growled and tossed Farger into a chair. Remo sat on the bed, facing him.

"I don't think we understand each other," Remo said. "I'm in this campaign to win. Not come close. Not make a good try. But win. And you seem to be approaching it with the idea of 'take the money and run.' "

The statement was an accusation and Farger answered it.

"What you don't understand," he said gingerly, feeling his way around the edges of Remo's annoyance, "is that we can't win."

"Why not? Everybody keeps telling me we can't win. Will somebody please tell me why?"

"Because we've got nothing going for us. Money, candidate, support. We got nothing."

"What kind of money do you need for a one-week campaign?"

"For printing, stunts, election day expenses, sound trucks, gimmicks, we'd need $100,000," Farger said.

"All right," Remo said. "You've got $200,000. Cash. And now I don't want any more crap about you couldn't do this or you couldn't afford that, or if you had more money, things would be different. Does that solve your problem?"

Farger blinked. He was already thinking as a lifetime in politics had trained him to think: how much of that loose campaign money he could skim off for himself. It took a few seconds before he could again focus his mind on the major problem.

"We need exposure," he said. "Advertising, commercials, brochures, signs for telephone poles. The whole thing."

"You got it," Remo said. "I hired the best ad agency in the world. Their girl will be here this afternoon. What else?"

Farger sighed. His native goodness vied with his greed. Finally the goodness won out and he decided to tell the truth, even if Remo did pack up his wallet and call off the whole campaign.

"No matter what you spend or what we do, we can't win. There's three things important in a campaign: the candidate, the candidate and the candidate. And we don't have one."

"Hogwash," Remo said. "Every campaign I ever saw, there were three important things all right: the money, the money and the money. And we've got the money and I'm giving you a blank check to use it. Just use it right."

"But recognition . . . respectability?"

"We get that the way politicians always do. Buy the news guys."

"But we don't have any support," Farger protested. "What about people? Workers? Endorsements? We don't have any. We've got you and me and those three chippies out there, and if I didn't give them their 300 bucks each in advance, they wouldn't be there either. I'm not even sure we've got Mac Polaney, because he's such a gone job, he's liable to vote for somebody else himself."

"Don't worry about that," Remo said. "Mac doesn't vote."

Farger groaned.

"What people do we need?" Remo asked.

"Leaders. Union people. Politicians."

"Give me a list."

"It won't help to talk to them. All of them are with Cartwright."

"You just give me a list. I can be very persuasive."

Remo stayed in headquarters, long enough to assure himself that Farger was seriously now tracking down phones and typewriters and copying equipment.

An hour later when Teri Walker arrived, Farger gave Remo the list of names, sent one of the girls to get Mac Polaney, and closeted himself with Teri to discuss the campaign, which now had only six days left to run.

CHAPTER FIFTEEN

Marshal Dworshansky watched the ice cubes drift gently in his glass, duplicating the smooth side to side movement of his yacht in the water, as he listened to the whining of Mayor Tim Cartwright.

"Farger left us," the mayor had just said. "That ingrate bastard. After all I did for him."

"What exactly did you do for him?" the marshal asked, raising his glass to his lips, and his heavy shoulders bunched up into knots of muscle under his lime colored silk shirt.

"What did I do? I didn't fire his dumb ass. For years, I've left him down there in the elections office, instead of kicking him out in the street."

"And you did it, of course, out of the goodness of your heart?" Dworshansky said.

"Damn near," Cartwright said. "Although he has been a loyal slob. The perfect guy to give shit jobs too."

"Aha," Dworshansky said. "You gave him a job; he gave you his support. An even trade, I would say. And now he has voided the contract. Perhaps he has gotten a better offer."

"Yeah, but campaign manager for Mac Polaney? What kind of offer is that?" He paused, then chuckled to himself. "He probably thinks Polaney's going to make him city treasurer. Polaney offers that job to everybody." He chuckled again. "Mac Polaney, running for mayor." He laughed aloud as if he found the thought unbearably funny. "Mac Polaney."

"You find him amusing?" Dworshansky asked.

"Marshal, there's an old rule in politics that goes: you

can't beat somebody with nobody. Mac Polaney's nobody."

"He has a very good advertising agency," the marshal said softly.

Cartwright laughed some more. "What kind of New York lunatic would take on Polaney's campaign?" he chortled.

"My daughter's advertising agency," Dworshansky said. "And they are very good. Probably the best in the world."

Cartwright found that reason enough to stop laughing.

"It is about time you have restrained your mirth," Dworshansky said. "Because this is a very serious matter."

He sipped his vodka delicately, and glanced out the cabin window as he began to speak.

"We have kept you out of jail with a smoke screen. To set it up, we had to dispose of that fool from the bank, and as I remember, you did not laugh then.

"I warned you that the government would not sit quietly by and allow this to happen; that their secret organization would fight back. We tied Farger to a post as a sacrificial lamb, and you did not laugh then. They frightened Farger as earlier they had frightened Mr. Moskowitz, whom it was necessary to un-frighten."

Dworshansky drained his glass in an angry gulp. "Now Farger means nothing to me, but he is the first chip in our defenses. And if our enemies choose to use this Mister Polaney as the instrument of their retaliation, then I would suggest sincerely that you stop laughing at Mr. Polaney, because it may not be long before he is dancing on your grave."

Cartwright looked hurt, and Dworshansky put down the glass, rose, and clapped the mayor on the shoulder.

"Come," he said. "Do not despair. We have infiltrated their campaign organization. We will guarantee that

Mr. Polaney does not win the election. And mostly we will just sit and wait, to see what our enemies do."

Cartwright looked up at Dworshansky and retreated behind his politician's mask. "You're a real friend," he said. "I can't tell you of the faith I have in you. Yes sir, a real friend."

"Well, that and more," said Dworshansky. "I am a real partner as you will find after you win. Of course, I know you would not forget that, just as you would not forget that I now have Bullingsworth's notebook."

Cartwright looked hurt. "Marshal, I won't forget your help. Really."

"I know you won't," Dworshansky said. "Now, in the meantime, I suggest that you campaign hard and leave Mr. Polaney and this Remo friend of his to me. But do not underestimate them. That way lies the boneyard."

CHAPTER SIXTEEN

The black and white killer whale swam around the large, kidney-shaped pool, slowly at first, then faster and faster as he built up speed and then, after four rounds of the pool, he jumped straight up, high out of the water, even his tail slapping only air, and with his tooth-lined mouth squeezed the rubber bulb on a horn hung high above the water's surface.

It honked. The honk hung in the air for a split second and then was overwhelmed by the crashing splash as the whale's tonnage slammed down flat against the water.

As he slid back down into the pool's depths, children laughed and the sun-baked crowd applauded. Chiun sat with Remo in a front row seat and said, "Barbarians."

"What now?" Remo asked.

"Why is it you white men think it somehow charming to take an animal, a creature of nature, put a ribbon on him and have him beep a horn? Is it cute?"

"Who's it hurt?" Remo said. "The whale doesn't even seem to mind."

Chiun turned to him, away from the pool where a pretty blonde was now riding around on the back of the whale. "You are, as usual, wrong. The spectacle hurts the whale because he is no longer free. And it hurts you because—senselessly, without considering the consequences—you haved deprived that animal of his freedom. It makes you less a man, because you no longer think and feel as a man.

"And look at these children. What are they learning here? How they too can one day grow up and imprison nature's beasts? Barbarians."

"As opposed to?"

"As opposed to anyone who does not tamper with the order of the universe. As opposed to anyone who appreciates the virtues of the free life."

"Strange to hear an assassin sing the praises of life."

Chiun exploded in a babble of excited Korean, then said, "Death is a part of life. It has always been thus. But it required you white men to discover something worse than death. The cage."

"You don't have zoos in Sinanju?"

"Yes," Chiun said evenly. "In them we keep Chinese and white men."

"All right," Remo said, "forget it. I just thought you'd like to see the aquarium. It's the most famous in the world."

"After lunch, may we visit the Black Hole of Calcutta?"

"Will it improve your disposition?"

"The Master of Sinanju spreads light wherever he walks."

"Right on, Chiun, right on." Remo was surprised at Chiun's display of ill humor. Since they had arrived in Miami Beach, the old man had been in great spirits. He talked to wealthy old Jewish ladies about the transgressions of their children. Mrs. Goldberg, he had breathlessly told Remo, had a son who had not visited her in three years. And Mrs. Hirshberg's son did not even telephone. Mrs. Kantrowitz had three sons, all doctors, and when her cat caught cold, not one of them would take the case, even though she would have insisted upon paying, so as not to be a burden.

Mrs. Milstein was the woman whose son was the television writer, and Chiun marvelled that she bore up so bravely under the disgrace of a son who wrote Chinese comedies. She did not even acknowledge disgrace, Chiun said, but walked with her head high. A sterling woman, he had said.

For his part, Chiun must also have talked about his son who would not carry the luggage and who embarrassed him at every turn. What he said, Romo could only guess by the fact that occasionally walking through the halls of their apartment, he was hissed by old ladies entering their own apartments. Chiun talked, too, of his desire to go back to the old country and see the village where he had been born. He would, he said, gladly have retired, but he did not feel that his son was yet able to carry on his work. Your son, my son, her son, their son. Chiun and the ladies talked. If any of them had ever given birth to a daughter, it was not mentioned.

In just a few days, Chiun seemed to have met half the Jewish Momma population of Miami Beach. He also seemed to be happy and Remo expected him to be happy for the chance to see the aquarium. He had not expected abuse.

Remo shrugged, took a sheet of yellow lined paper from his shirt pocket, and looked at it again.

"C'mon, Chiun," he said. "Our man works at the shark run."

The shark run was a half-mile-long oval of shallow water. In a half-dozen places, the narrow channel broadened out into deep pools and jagged rock inlets. The entire run was bordered by a steel fence, over which spectators could lean and look down at the sharks swimming by. There were hundreds of sharks in the run, of all sizes and shapes and types. With the maniacal single-mindedness of the deadly, they ignored the wide spots in the run, they ignored the deep pools. Instead, they just swam continuously around, oval after oval, mile after mile, a ceaseless search for something to kill.

The only break in their routine was feeding time, when the fishes and the red meat thrown into the water drove them into frenzies that turned the water white and bubbly as they fought for their meals, not with their jaws and teeth, but like basketball players fighting for a rebound, with their bodies and their stealth.

The first name on Remo's list was Damiano Meola, head of the county's government employees union. Meola and the two thousand employees of the union already had backed Mayor Cartwright for reelection.

Chiun and Remo found him in a sheltered, shaded area in the back of the shark run, a small section sealed off from the public by a locked gate. Meola was a big man, his burly body pulling at the seams of his light blue workmen's uniform. He stood at the rail of the shark run, large buckets of dead fish at his feet, dropping them one at a time into the water, and laughing as the water churned into froth just below him.

He talked to himself as he fed his charges. "Go get it. That's right, sweetheart. Take it away from him. Watch out for Mako. Careful. Don't let that mother get it. Careful. Ahh, what's the matter? Hungry? Starve, you vicious bastard!"

He reached down to pick up another fish, and then stopped, as he saw behind him Remo and Chiun's feet. He turned around quickly, an angry expression on his broad, flat-featured face. "Hey, wotsamatta witcha, this part ain't open to the public. G'wan, scram."

"Mister Meola?" Remo asked politely.

"Yeah. Watcha want?"

"We've come to talk to you."

"Yeah?"

"We represent Mr. Mac Polaney."

"Yeah?"

"And we want you to support him."

Meola laughed in their faces. "Mac Polaney!" he said sputtering. "Hah. That's a laugh."

Remo waited quietly until he had finished laughing. Chiun stood, his hands folded inside the sleeves of his thin yellow robe, his eyes looking skyward.

Finally, when Meola had quieted down, Remo said, "We're not joking."

"Well, for people who ain't joking, you sure tell funny stories. Mac Polaney. G'wan, get out of here." He turned away, picked up a dead fish by its tail and held it out over the water.

Remo stepped to one side of him and Chiun to the other.

"Mind telling me why you're against Polaney?" Remo asked.

"Because my members endorsed Cartwright."

"But your members do what you tell them. Why not Polaney?" Remo asked.

"Because he's a screwball is why."

"Two thousand dollars," Remo said.

Meola stopped and shook his head. He dropped the fish into the water and the sharks attacked.

"Five thousand dollars," Remo said.

Meola shook his head again.

"Name a price," Remo said.

Meola, thinking of his brother-in-law, who was a stockbroker handling all the assets of the employees' pension fund and splitting his earnings with Meola, said, "No price, never, nothing. Now, get out of here because you're starting to annoy me."

"Ever see a man bitten by a shark?" Remo asked.

"Watch this," Meola said. "It drives them crazy." He took a fish from the bucket and with a knife he carried in a sheath on his side, slit its belly open. He dropped the gutted carcass into the water. Instant explosion as the sharks went berserk.

"It must be the smell or something," Meola said. "But gut a fish and they go wild."

"How long do you think a man could last in there?" Meola dropped in another fish.

"A man with gutted fish in his pockets and cuffs?" Remo said.

"Hey. You threatening me? 'Cause if you are, I'm gonna call the cops. 'Cause I don't like you. You and your dinko friend."

He opened to his mouth to say something else, but he could not get a word out because a fish was jammed deep into his mouth by Chiun. Meola gagged and tried to spit, but Chiun slapped the fish deeper. Meola reached up to pull it out, and Remo pinched both his wrists. Meola found he could not raise his arms.

"Time to test your theory, Meola," said Remo. He slipped the knife from Meola's sheath, and began to slit the gullets of fish from the bucket. He slipped one into Meola's right trouser pocket and another into his left. A third he stuck inside Meola's shirt, and two more went into Meola's cuffs.

Meola moaned through the fish gag. He shook his head from side to side, his eyes widened in fear. Then he tried to run, but the two men stopped him. Somehow, they stopped him with just one finger each.

And then Meola found himself being lifted by the shirt collar and held out over the deep pool. He looked down and between his suspended feet, he could see the sleek brown and gray bodies of the sharks, slipping back and forth noiselessly through the water, searching.

He heard the white man talking. "Mac Polaney is a decorated veteran. He has broad political experience. He is incorruptible. He is just the man our city needs to lead it through these perilous times. Don't you agree?"

Meola failed to nod.

He felt his body dip and then water slipped into his shoes, before he was yanked upward again, a foot above the water.

"All our loyal government employees want is decent government, a chance to do an honest day's work for an honest day's pay. Isn't that right?"

Meola nodded and as reward felt himself lifted a few inches higher.

"Upon reconsideration, as president of the employees' union, you feel that Mac Polaney's election will be a great step forward for the people of Miami Beach. Do I quote you accurately?"

Meola nodded frantically. How long could this guy hold him out over the water, before his arm tired and Meola was dropped?

Meola nodded. Again and again.

He felt himself being lifted effortlessly, swooped up over the railing and placed back on the ground.

The white man pulled the fish from his mouth.

"I'm glad you saw it our way," he said. "Mac Polaney'll be glad to have you aboard."

Remo reached into his pocket and took out a stack of papers that Farger had prepared. He leafed through them, found the one he wanted and replaced the others.

Remo glanced over it, then nodded to himself. "Sign here," he said. "It's an endorsement. You want to read it?"

Meola shook his head. His voice came back, but his throat still hurt. "No, no," he said. "Anything you want."

"Good," Remo said. He took Meola's pen, clicked it and handed it to him. "Sign."

Meola tried to reach for the pen, but his arms would not move. "My arms," he said.

"Oh," Remo said. He reached forward with his right hand and pressed Meola's wrists, first the right, then the left. Immediately, Meola felt control and strength moving back into his arms.

"Now sign," said Remo, handing forward the paper and pencil.

Meola signed and handed them back. Remo checked the signature, folded the paper and put it in his pocket. He replaced the pen in the breast pocket of Meola's blue work shirt.

Remo met his eyes. "All right," he said, "now I know

what you're thinking. You're thinking that as soon as we leave, you're going to call the cops. Or else you're going to retract the endorsement, and call it a hoax. That's what you're thinking. But that's not what you're going to do. Because if you do, we're going to come back and feed you to your playmates. Count on it. That's solid gold. Chiun."

Remo nodded to Chiun and the old man leaned forward and picked up one of the fish from the pail. As Meola watched, the delicate Oriental tossed the foot-long fish into the air. As it came down, his hands flashed through the air, glinting in the sun like golden knife blades. When the fish hit the ground, it had been cut into three pieces by Chiun's hands.

Meola looked at the fish, then at the old man, who had again folded his hands inside the sleeves of his robe.

"We'll dismember you like that fish," Remo said. "Piece by piece, and then we'll feed the pieces to the sharks."

He put a hand on Meola's shoulder and for the first time, Meola noticed how thick the man's wrists were. "Are you afraid?" Remo asked.

Meola nodded.

"Good," Remo said. "You'd better be scared to death."

He took his hand from Meola's shoulder, took a piece of yellow paper from his shirt pocket and looked at it. "Come on, Chiun," he said, "we've got more visits to make."

They turned to walk away, but Remo stopped and turned back to Meola. "I'm glad you saw it our way. Rest easy. You're doing the best thing for the city. Cross us and there won't be enough left of you to get a hook into."

Remo turned, put his arm around Chiun's shoulder and walked away. Meola heard him say, "See, Chiun.

Reasonable minds can always reach political compromises."

Meola looked at them, then down at the fish which the Oriental's flying hands had slashed into bits.

Why not Mac Polaney? he thought. After all, he was a decorated veteran with broad political experience; he was incorruptible; and he had *some* kind of campaign volunteers.

CHAPTER SEVENTEEN

Lt. Chester Grabnick, head of the Uniformed Officers Association, was an honest cop.

In seventeen years as a policeman, he had not taken money from gamblers, he had not protected narcotics dealers, he had not indulged in brazen brutality.

There had been just one tiny little mistake.

"When you were a rookie patrolman, you used to steal reports from the detective bureau and turn them over to a defense lawyer."

The man who brought him this news was in his thirties and he had a hard face. He tried to turn the face softer now as he said, "It would be a shame to ruin a good career for that sort of youthful indiscretion."

Grabnick was silent, thinking.

Finally, he said, "You got the wrong guy."

"No, I haven't," his visitor said. "I have an affidavit from the laywer."

Chester Grabnick, who was the lawyer's best friend and who bowled with him every Wednesday night, said, "You do? How could you get a thing like that?"

"It was easy," the man said. "I broke his arm."

Without much more discussion, Lt. Chester Grabnick decided that the election of Mac Polaney would be the best thing that could ever happen to Miami Beach and its loyal, dedicated force of men in blue.

"Will your membership go along?" his visitor asked.

"They'll go along," Grabnick said, sure of himself. His success had been built upon the reputation of "Honest Chet." So long as nothing happened to damage that reputation, he could get the uniformed officers to back anybody he wanted.

"Good," his visitor said. "Make sure you do."

In the car outside Grabnick's home, Remo slid behind the wheel and said to Chiun, "All right. We got him. That's two. A good day's work."

"I do not understand," Chiun said. "Will people vote for your candidate because this policeman tells them to?"

"That's the theory," Remo said. "Get the leaders and the peasants fall in line."

"But one can never tell about peasants," Chiun said. "That is why they are peasants. I remember once. . . ."

Remo sighed. Another history lesson.

CHAPTER EIGHTEEN

"Here's your first two," said Remo, tossing the endorsements on Farger's desk at campaign headquarters.

Farger picked up the papers, read them quickly, double-checked the signatures, then looked up at Remo with renewed respect.

"How'd you do it?" he asked.

"We reasoned together. Teri still here?"

"Inside," Farger said, jerking a thumb over his shoulder. "Busy as a beaver."

Teri Walker sat behind a large metal desk, its top festooned with pads, pencils, paper, sketches. She wore large, owlish dark-framed eyeglasses, pushed up on top of her head and she smiled at Remo as he came in the door.

"I met the candidate," she said. "You know we're going to win?"

"All that confidence from one meeting with the candiate? What did he say?"

"He said I had beautiful ears."

"Ears?"

"Ears. And he said if I'd run away on his houseboat with him, he'd retire from public life and spent the rest of his days showering my feet with catfish."

"That's truly touching," Remo said. "And that proves we're going to win the election?"

"Don't you see, Remo, I believed him. That's what we've got with our candidate. Believability. And he's . . . well, nice is the only word for it. So our advertising is going to be all about that—a nice, sweet guy that you can believe. Studies show that in politics, the voter, taken as a group overall and not subdivided into its minor ethnic or socio-economic components, well, that average voter wants . . ."

"Sure," Remo said. "When do we start our commercials, our advertising?"

"Well, we don't have time to do anything really fancy with either. But mother is flying down two staff people. We're going to go with just one TV commercial for the whole campaign. That starts tomorrow. Absolute saturation. The newspaper ads start the next day. How much do we have to spend, by the way?"

Remo said, "I'll send over a couple of hundred thousand. When that's done, ask for more."

She looked at him quizzically but approvingly. "When you go, you go," she said.

"Anything for honest government," Remo said.

"Is it your money?" she asked—just a little too casually, Remo noted.

"Of course," Remo said. "Who'd give me money to spend on Mac Polaney? Only somebody as nutty as Mac himself, and people that nutty aren't rich, or if they are, all their money is tied up in hospitals for homeless cats."

"There's a logical nonsequitur there, but I can't figure it out," she said.

"Don't try. If I were logical, do you think I'd be financing Mac's campaign? Where is the next mayor, by the way?"

"Oh, he went back to his boat. He's repairing some rods for the annual catfish contest next week."

"Next week? It's not on election day, is it?"

"I don't think so. Why?"

"If it is, Mac might not even get his own vote," Remo said.

She smiled, slightly patronizing, as if she were able to read depths in Mac Polaney's soul that eluded a crass beast like Remo, and went back to work. Remo watched her for awhile, grew bored and left.

Farger still sat at the front desk, but he had an unhappy look on his face. Remo did not know whether that was because the three so-called secretaries had left for the day, or because tragedy had befallen the campaign. So he asked.

"We got trouble," Farger said. "The paper won't use these endorsements."

"Why not?"

Farger ran his fingertips together indicating money. "The same reason the paper only used one line about me becoming Polaney's campaign manager. Me . . . who is front page news around the country. It's the political reporter. Tom Burns. He's on Cartwright's pad. His wife's a no-show crossing guard and he's a no-show truant officer."

"No-show?"

"Yeah. He gets the paycheck but doesn't show up for work. Anyway, the little bastard told me the endorsements weren't news. He forgets that last week, when the same people endorsed Cartwright, they were front page news." He slammed a pencil down on his desk. "If we can't get the endorsements in, how are we going to create any movement?"

"We'll get them in," Remo said.

He found Tom Burns in a cocktail lounge around the corner from the editorial officers of the *Miami Beach Dispatch,* the city's biggest and most influential paper.

Burns was a little man with graying hair that he touched up to keep black. Thick horn-rimmed glasses covered his vague-looking eyes. He wore cuffed pants and a jacket with frayed sleeves. Although the bar was crowded, he sat by himself, and Remo knew enough about reporters to know that if Burns had been even bearable, he would have had a crowd of publicity-seekers around him, particularly in the middle of an election campaign.

So much for Burns' personality.

He was drinking Harvey's Bristol Cream on the rocks. He couldn't drink either.

Remo slid into a stool at his left, and said politely, "Mr. Burns?"

"Yes," Burns said, coldly, distantly.

"My name is Harold Smith. I'm with a special Senate Committee investigating coercion of the free press. Do you have a minute?"

"I suppose so," Burns said laconically, trying to mask his pleasure about being asked for his opinion on encroachment on news gathering, the right of a reporter to conceal his sources, the necessity of protecting the First Amendment. But how could he say all that in a minute?

He turned out to have more than a minute, and he didn't talk at all. He only listened. He listened as the man explained that the Senate was interested in cases where politicians had tried "to buy" members of the press, in order to insure favorable news coverage. "Do you know, Mr. Burns, that there are newspapermen who not only have themselves but their relatives on public payrolls, drawing salaries without doing work?" This Harold Smith seemed horrified at the thought. Burns learned that Mr. Harold Smith was tracking down just such a reporter in the Miami Beach area, and Mr. Harold Smith was going to subpoena that reporter to testify before a public Senate hearing in Washington, D. C., and maybe, even, indict him. No, Mr. Burns, it would not be difficult to find him, because all Mr. Harold Smith had to do was to read the local press and find out which reporter is not giving fair coverage to the opponents of the incumbent. That would be the right reporter.

Oh, Mr. Burns had to go? Oh, he had to write several stories about new endorsements of Mr. Mac Polaney? Oh, tell it like it is, had always been his motto?

Well, that's really wonderful, Mr. Burns. More reporters should be like you. That was Mr. Harold Smith's feeling. He looked forward to reading Mr. Burns' wonderful coverage of Mr. Mac Polaney for the remainder of the campaign.

Burns left without leaving a tip for the bartender. Remo shoveled a five dollar bill onto the bar. That was the cheapest he'd gotten off in anything he'd done in this campaign.

CHAPTER NINETEEN

The newspaper the next morning had headlined the defections from Cartwright's camp to Mac Polaney. Under Burns' by-line, the story said that what appeared to have been merely a coronation ceremony for the incumbent mayor might now grow into a horse race.

Another story quoted Cartwright in another attack on the federal government, for trying to interfere with the municipal election. Cartwright said that "vast sums" of money had been shipped from Washington for use by his opponents, in an effort to beat him because he would not be Washington's toady. From the start, Cartwright said, with the infamous League Papers, it was apparent that Washington was trying to dictate to Miami Beach its choice of a mayor.

Another story on Page One was datelined Washington. It quoted the President's press secretary as saying that a full investigation was underway into the League papers, and that a report should be on the President's desk when he returned from his Summit meeting next week. The story cheered Remo; it meant he had a few more days in which to bail out CURE.

Remo put down the paper and chuckled to Chiun, "We're going to win this thing."

Chiun sat, in his blue meditative robe, and looked slowly and quizzically at Remo.

"That is your opinion?" he asked.

"It is."

"Then heaven help us, because the fools have taken over the asylum."

"Now, what's eating you?"

"What do you know of politics, my son, that you can say now we will do this, or now we will do that? Why do you not understand the simple wisdom of finding a new emperor? It is as if you were one of those Chinese priests in that terrible television tale, dedicating yourself to social work."

"You know very well, Chiun, I'm involved in this to try to save Smith and the organization that pays the freight for you and me."

"I have watched you now. You have this Mr. Farger, who is as imperfect a human being as could be found. You have this Miss Walker, who is practicing at your expense. So I say to you, if you must do this thing, why do you not call in an expert?"

"Because, Chiun, in this country no one knows anything about politics. The experts least of all. That's why there still is an American dream. Because the whole system is so nutty that every nut has a chance to win. Even Mac Polaney. Even with me running things for him."

Chiun turned away. "Call Dr. Smith," he said.

"What would you have me call him?"

"Do not fear, my son, that you will ever drown in your arrogance. For surely, before that day arrives, you will have choked on your ignorance."

"You stick with me, Chiun," Remo said. "How'd you like to be city treasurer?"

But Chiun's remarks rankled. Remo had gotten into politics to force Cartwright's people to come after him, since he was unable to attack Cartwright head-on. And yet, nothing had happened. No one had moved, and it forced him to wonder, against his will, if he was even in the ball game. He would not take many more pitches, he thought, before he started swinging.

The big name on Remo's list for the day was Nick Bazzani, who was the leader of the Miami Beach northern ward. Remo and Chiun found him in his ward club, snuggled into a side street under a large red and white sign that proclaimed "Cartwright for Mayor. North Ward Civic Association, Nick Bazzani, Standard-Bearer."

"What's a standard-bearer?" Remo asked Chiun.

"He carries the flag in the annual parade of ragamuffins," Chiun said, looking with distaste around the main clubroom where men in tee shirts sat in wooden chairs, drinking beer and talking.

"What can I do for you?" one man asked Remo, looking curiously at Chiun.

"Nick Bazzani. I want to see him."

"He's busy now. Make an appointment," the man said, jerking his thumb toward a door that apparently led to a back room.

"He'll see us," Remo said, brushing past the man and leading Chiun through the door, into the backroom.

The room was a small office with a desk, extra chairs, and a small table on which sat a portable color television set.

There were three men in the room. Bazzani apparently was the one behind the desk. He was fattish and red-haired; he had that dumb look that only red-headed Italians are able to master fully. Remo put his age in his late thirties. The other two men in the room were younger, dark-haired, much impressed by being close to Bazzani, who was probably the most wonderful, grandest man they had ever hoped to meet.

"Hey, this is a private office," one of the men said.

"That's good," Remo said. "My business is private." He turned to the man at the desk. "Bazzani?"

"Shhhh," said the man. "It's coming on now."

He was staring at the television set. Remo and Chiun turned to watch. The game show emcee said, "We'll be back in just one minute."

"Shhhh now, everybody," Bazzani said.

A soap commercial came on.

"It's next," Bazzani said.

The soap commercial died, there was a moment of blank air, and then on screen came a large sunflower, with a hole in its center. It filled the screen in garish color for a few seconds and then, into the hole in the center, popped the head of Mac Polaney.

Remo winced.

Polaney seemed fixed there for a moment, then opened his mouth and began to sing, to the plinking of one banjo accompaniment:

"Sunshine is nicer.

Flowers are sweeter.

We need a man

to clean up the town."

It went on and on and ended with:

"Vote for Polaney.

Early and Often."

Bazzani had giggled when the sunflower first came on the screen. He laughed aloud when he saw Polaney's face. At the end of the jingle, he was roaring. Tears streamed down his cheeks. He tried hard to catch his breath.

The song ended, and over the sunflower and Polaney's face came a printed legend:

"Sunshine is Nicer.

Vote for Polaney."

Then the commercial faded and the game show came back on. Bazzani was still convulsed. Through tears and gasps, he managed to sing:

"Vote for Polaney,

He is a hoople."

Then off into more laughter, demanding of everybody in the room, "Did you see that? Did you see that?"

Remo and Chiun stood silently in the middle of the floor, waiting.

It took a full sixty seconds before Bazzani could catch

his breath and regain some of his composure. Finally, he looked up at Remo and Chiun and wiped away the tears of mirth which sparkled on his fat, meaty face.

"Can I help you?" he asked.

"Yes," Remo said. "We're from Mr. Polaney's headquarters, and we've come to ask your support."

Bazzani chuckled as if a partner to a joke.

Remo said nothing. Bazzani looked at him, waiting for him to say more. But when Remo said nothing, he finally asked in surprise, *"Whose* headquarters?"

"Mac Polaney," Remo said. "The next mayor of Miami Beach."

This pronouncement was good for another thirty seconds of general hilarity, this time shared by Bazzani's two companions.

"Why do they laugh?" Chiun asked Remo. "Mister Polaney is correct. Sunshine is nicer."

"I know," Remo said, "but some people don't have any feel for truth and beauty."

Bazzani showed no sign of ever letting up. Every time he stopped laughing to catch his breath, he hissed "Mac Polaney," then he and his two spear carriers were off again.

Perhaps if Remo got his attention. He stepped forward to the desk which was bare except for a newspaper opened to the race results, a telephone and a metal bust of Robert E. Lee.

Remo lifted the statue in his left hand and put his right hand on top of its head. He wrenched with his hands and ripped off the bronze head. Bazzani stopped laughing and watched. Remo dropped the rest of the bust and put both hands to the top of the skull in his right hand. He twisted and wrenched, moving his hands back and forth in unfamiliar patterns, his fingers moving individually as if tapping on different keys. Then he opened his hand and let bronze dust and flakes to which he had reduced the statue dribble between his fingers onto Bazzani's desk.

Bazzani stopped laughing. His mouth hung open. He seemed unable to remove his eyes from the pile of bronze metallic dust on his desk blotter.

"And now that Laugh-in is over," Remo said, "we're going to talk about your endorsement of Mac Polaney."

The words jolted Bazzani to attention. "Alfred," he said. "Rocco. Get these two nuts out of here."

"Chiun," Remo said softly, his back still turned to the other two men.

They moved toward Remo. Behind him, he heard two sharp cracks as if boards were breaking, and then two thumps as bodies hit the floor.

"Now that we won't be interrupted," Remo said, "why have you been supporting Cartwright?"

"He's the city leader. I always support the city leader," Bazzani said. His voice was still loud and blustery, but there was a new note in it now. One of fear.

"So did Meola and Lt. Grabnick," Remo said. "But they saw the light. They're supporting Polaney now."

"But I can't," Bazzani whined. "My membership. . . ."

"But you must," Remo said. "And forget your membership. Are you their leader or not?"

"Yeah, but. . . ."

"No buts," Remo said. "Look, I'll make it clear for you. Support Polaney and you get $5,000 and you keep breathing. Tell me no, and your head's going to look like Robert E. Lee's there."

Bazzani looked down at the pile of dust again, then sputtered, "I never heard of such a thing. Politics isn't done this way."

"Politics is always done this way. I've just eliminated the middle step of beating around the bush. Well? What's the answer? You want to be with Polaney, or you want to have your skull caved in?"

Bazzani, for the first time, searched Remo's eyes and

found nothing in there but truth. It was hard to believe that this was happening to him, but for the life of him, he couldn't figure out anything to do. He looked past Remo down at the floor, where Rocco and Albert lay still.

"They're not dead," Remo said, "but they could just as easily have been. All right, time's up." He took a step toward the desk.

"What do you want me to do?" Bazzani said, with a sigh.

Before Rocco and Albert regained consciousness, Remo had Bazzani's signature on an endorsement and Bazzani had Remo's five thousand dollars in his pocket.

"A fair trade," Remo said, "is a bargain for everyone. One last thing."

Bazzani looked up.

"How'd you know Polaney's commercial was going to be on?"

"We got a list of all the times they're running."

"From who?"

"Cartwright's headquarters."

"Okay," Remo said, with a small smile. "Now don't cross me. Mr. Polaney's happy to have you aboard."

He turned, stepped over Rocco and Alfred and led Chiun out, through the front clubrooms and out into the street.

He was worried, but happy. Bazzani had had the list of commercials and they had come from Cartwright. That meant that Cartwright had a pipeline into Polaney's campaign organization, and that was cause for worry. But it also made Remo happy, because it meant that the Cartwright people were moving. Slowly—true, but they were moving . . . toward Remo.

His concentration was broken by Chiun's voice. He turned. Chiun was singing softly under his breath:

"Sunshine is nicer.

"Flowers are sweeter."

CHAPTER TWENTY

"Did you see those commercials?"

Willard Farger seemed pained. He sat at his desk in the main room of their campaign led headquarters suite, watching his three Playboy bunnies who seemed to be watching their fingernails grow.

"Yeah," said Remo. "What'd you think?"

"I thought they were terrible," Farger said. "Who's going to vote for a guy with his head in a sunflower?"

"History is full of elections where people voted for guys with their heads in their ass," Remo said. "Don't worry about it. It's all been carefully calculated and computed on Madison Avenue. And would they lie to us?"

Both he and Farger knew the answer to that question so it was not necessary to answer it. Instead, Remo said, "By the way, I don't mean to tell you your business, but shouldn't there be more people in headquarters than you and your harem? I mean, aren't there supposed to be real live voters around here who would die or cheat or rob or kill for our candidate?"

Farger shrugged his shoulders. "Sure there are. Where do I get them?"

"I thought they came after we got the endorsements from Meola and Grabnick and Nick Bazzani," Remo said.

"Not enough," Farger said. "We get people when he prove we got a candidate who can win. It's like farming. You got to have seeds before you have plants. Well, the seeds are the first people. And you've got to have them to get in the other people who really work for you."

"The plants?"

"Right," Farger said.

"Well, how do you get those first people? The seeds?"

"You get them usually from the candidate himself. His friends, his family. They're the start of his organization. Our guy doesn't even have that. What's he going to do: staff headquarters with catfish?"

"It doesn't make any sense," Remo said. "We can't win unless we have people. And we can't get people, unless we prove we can win. Where does it start or end for that matter? What about the commercials? Will they help?"

Farger shook his head. "Not those commercials."

"The newspaper stories and ads?"

"Maybe a little. But we don't have time to build an organization by dribs and drabs."

"All right," Remo said. "It's decided."

"What is?" Farger asked.

"People. We need 'em. We're going to hire 'em."

"Hire them? Where are you going to hire people for a campaign?"

"I don't know. We've got to think about it. But that's the answer. Hire 'em."

"Hmmm," Farger said, musing. Then finally, "It might work. It just might." He paused as Teri Walker stepped out of her office, saw Remo, and smiled her way to him at Farger's desk.

"Did you see the commercials?" she asked.

"Sure did."

"And?"

"The one I saw was so effective a Cartwright ward leader switched over on the spot. Never saw a commercial with more pulling power than that one."

"You mark my words," Teri said. "The whole town will know Mac Polaney in the next forty-eight hours."

"What does your mother think?" Remo asked.

"I'd love to take the credit, but she's the one who gave me the idea. For the sunflower setting."

"And the song?"

"That came right from the candidate. He wrote it himself. He's sweet. He really believes it."

"So do I," Remo said. "Sunshine is nicer. We've just been talking about our manpower problems. We're thinking of hiring campaign workers."

"Sounds like a good idea," she said.

Farger said, "Our biggest problem is going to be election day at the polls. If we don't man every polling place, Cartwright's people will kill us. They'll steal our votes."

Remo nodded sagely although he had no idea how one would go about stealing a vote in this day and age of voting machines.

"How many people would you need?" he asked.

"At least two hundred."

"Two hundred people at $300 for the week. Sixty thousand," Remo said.

"Yeah. A lot of scratch."

"We've got it," Remo said. "Don't worry about it. All we've got to do is figure out where to get two hundred people in a hurry."

He left that problem with Farger and joined Teri Walker in her office where she showed him the layouts for the newspaper ads which would start running the next day. They showed Mac Polaney's head inside a sunflower, and the simple legend:

"Sunshine is Nicer.

"Vote for Polaney."

"What about issues?" Remo asked. "Taxes, air pollution, crime?"

She shook her head, tossing her long blonde hair lightly around her bare shoulders. "It won't work."

"Why?"

"Have you heard his positions? Take parking, for example. I asked him about parking. He said the whole thing was very simple. Cut down the parking meters and attach springs to their bases, then give them out to the public for use as pogo sticks. This, you see, would stop the theft of money from the meters, the vandalism of the meters themselves, and ease the traffic problem by getting people out of their cars and onto their pogo sticks. And then, there is air pollution. You know what his solution is to air pollution?"

"What?" Remo asked reluctantly.

"Zen breathing. He said air pollution is only a problem if you breathe. But if you practice zen breathing, you can cut down the number of breaths you take per minute. Cut them in half. This cuts the air pollution problem in half, without the expenditure of one cent by the public. And then there was crime. Do you really want to hear his position on law and order?"

"Not really," Remo said. "Stick with 'Sunshine is Nicer.' "

"That was my mother's advice and my grandfather's too. And they know what they're doing."

Remo nodded pleasantly at the insult, but was glum again as he got into the elevator for downstairs. But his spirits perked up as he heard the elevator operator humming under his breath thes melody of "Sunshine is Nicer."

Chiun could tell Remo was worried. "You are bothered?" he said.

"I need two hundred people to work on Polaney's campaign."

"And you do not know two hundred people?"

"No."

"And you do not know where to get that many strangers?"

"No."

"Can you not advertise in the little print in your newspapers?"

"Farger says I can't. It would destroy our image by admitting that we couldn't get campaign workers."

"Truly a problem," Chiun said.

"Truly," Remo agreed.

"But you will not call Dr. Smith?"

"No. I'm going to do this myself, Chiun. And that's one Smitty's going to owe me."

Chiun turned away, shaking his head.

The next morning, the problem became academic.

There was a Page One story in the *Miami Beach Dispatch* in which Mayor Cartwright attacked the mysterious forces behind his opposition, and charged that his primary opponents was planning "to import goons—professional, paid political hessians—to come into our city to disrupt our way of life."

Remo crumpled the paper and tossed it angrily to the floor.

There it was again, proof of Cartwright's pipeline into the Polaney camp. And this time Remo knew who it was.

Farger just had not been able to play it straight; he didn't have the guts to break loose from his old organization, and so he played double agent, taking Remo's money and tipping off Cartwright on what Polaney was doing.

Well, enough was enough. Farger would pay for it now.

So Remo thought. But Farger was to escape punishment at his hands.

CHAPTER TWENTY-ONE

Dr. Harold W. Smith, looked at the telephone for the hundredth time that morning, then stood and walked to the door of his office.

Ignoring his confidential secretary, his administrative assistant, and a string of other project assistants, he walked through their offices, out through a cluster of big open offices, and toward a side door of the main sanitarium building. Some of the workers at desks in the big offices stared at his departing figure in disbelief. But for a glimpse at lunch, they had never seen him except behind his desk. He was at his desk in the morning when they arrived; as often as not, he ate lunch there; and he worked late into the night, hours past the departure time of the Civil Service personnel who sat in the outer offices doing paper work on educational and medical research projects which served as Folcroft's cover. Some had never conceived of the idea of Dr. Smith walking anywhere; now to see him ambulating was a shock indeed.

There were two basic reasons Smith rarely left his desk. First, he was a compulsive worker. Work was his wife, his life, his mistress and his madness. Second, he resented any time spent away from his telephone, because over that telephone he learned of the problems CURE faced, and over that same bank of phones he could set into motion the world-wide apparatus that CURE had slowly accreted to itself over the past decade or more.

But now, he did not expect the phone to ring. The President was in Vienna at the Summit. He would not be back for several more days and Smith had that much time left before the President's last order to CURE became operational: Disband. Not that Smith would need to hear the order spoken. The instant he felt that CURE could not be saved; that its security was irrevocably breeched; that its continued existence was a disservice to the country; at that moment, Smith would act. It was a mark of his character that he did not regard his willingness to do that as a mark of character. It was the right thing to do; therefore, it was the kind of thing a man must do.

But now, as the day grew closer, he found himself asking the question of himself. Would he really scuttle CURE and take his own life in the process? He had never doubted it before, but that was when it had been just an academic possibility. Now, it approached reality. He wondered if he would indeed have the nerve.

Still, the question might not be put to him. There was still Remo.

He knew Remo would not telephone. He resisted calling on simple assignments; on this one, where Smith had lifted the need for reporting regularly, Remo would not call at all.

He was not overly optimistic about Remo's chances to nip the scandal of The League Papers in the bud. At the subtle cat and mouse games, Remo was as a child. And now, he was in the trickiest of all arenas—urban politics. CURE's mask had been torn because of politics, the need of Cartwright to block the investigation and indictments of his administration. The problem required a political solution, and Smith could tell, from reading the Florida papers, that Remo had moved into the political arena with a man named Polaney.

It was the right strategy, but Remo was the wrong tactician. Politics was a game with just too many finesses for the one-time cop.

Still, what else could Smith do but wait? When all was

said and done, when its millions of dollars and thousands of secret workers were counted and recounted, CURE was two people—Smith, the head, and Remo, the hand. Nothing else. No one else.

Smith strolled to the shore of the sound, where the ground gently broke away and leaned down into the water, baring stones polished smooth by the pounding of the water, glistening now gold and silver in the morning sunlight.

The waves lapped gently at the incline, and Smith looked at the nearest wave, then one behind it, then one farther out, until finally he was looking out across the broad expanse of Long Island Sound. He had looked at it for years: when CURE was just an idea, and when it was a reality; when its missions were simple and when they were complex. The water gave him the feeling of permanence in a jerry-built world. But now he understood that the permanence of the water belonged only to the water. CURE had come and CURE could go. Dr. Harold W. Smith had lived and Dr. Harold W. Smith would die. But the waves would roll, and more and more pebbles would go smooth and round, to be polished gold and silver by the waves.

If the sea never changed, was CURE worth having created? Was it worth it for Dr. Harold W. Smith to have left a lifetime of honored government service to head the mission, because a now-dead president had told him he was the only man for the job?

Smith asked himself that question as he looked now at the water, but he knew his answer. It was the answer that had sustained him for years, through all the pushing of buttons that had somehow cost other men their lives. Each man does what he can and each man's effort counts. There was no reason for life if a man did not believe that.

Perhaps even Remo knew that. It could explain why he had gone to Miami Beach instead of fleeing, which was what Smith expected him to do. And if he had gone on the assignment . . . well, then he might just call.

Smith scaled a rock at the water, then turned and went back inside, to sit at the telephone.

But Remo had other things on his mind, besides Dr. Harold W. Smith. For one, Willard Farger.

Farger was not at campaign headquarters. Roused long enough to be coherent, one of the bunny-secretaries confided to Remo that Farger had come in uncharacteristically early, gotten a phone message and left.

"He ain't gonna be late getting back, is he?" she said, snapping her gum as she talked. "I was going to use today's check to go shopping at lunch hour?"

"Today's check?"

She nodded. "Farger pays us by the day. He thinks that's the only way we'd show up. But I'd show up anyway, just to see you. You're cute."

"You're cute, too," Remo said. "Do you know who the phone message was from?"

The girl looked at a pad on her desk. "Here it is," she said. "This party called early, and left the number. When Farger came in, he called it an left."

She gave Remo the number and turned away, humming, "Sunshine is Nicer."

Remo went to Farger's desk and dialed the number. "Mayor Cartwright's headquarters," a female voice answered. Even though it was early in the day, in the background Remo could hear the buzz of excited voices, typewriters pounding, other telephones ringing. Remo held the phone to his ear for a moment, listening, and ruefully contemplating the three bunnies in the Mac Polaney Campaign Hutch. Then, angrily, he hung up.

Double-agent Farger. Gone, no doubt, to report to Cartwright how he was taking the smartass easterner's money and was sinking the Polaney campaign.

Why had he ever gotten involved in this? Remo wondered. Why? What did he know about politics? The dumbest green kid from a ward club would have handled himself smarter than Remo had. His first impulse had been right. Knock off Cartwright. Stick to what he knew. And what he knew was death.

First, Farger's.

Cartwright's headquarters were in another hotel on the Miami Beach strip, five long blocks away.

"He was here earlier," a bright-faced, young girl told Remo, "but he left."

The office was a maelstrom of activity and people and noise.

"Think you're going to win?" Remo asked the girl.

"Certainly," the girl said. "Mayor Cartwright is a fine man. It takes one to stand up to the fascist pigs in Washington."

Suddenly, Remo realized a great truth. There were no real reasons why anyone supported a political candidate, not logical ones anyway. People voted their stupidities, and then justified them by seeing in their chosen candidate what they wanted to see.

Like the girl. A government-hater, she cast Cartwright in that mold, and made it the most important part of his makeup. Logic, obviously, had no part in it because if it had, she would certainly have supported Polaney, whose election was a guarantee of instant anarchy.

Democracy was a statistical accumulation of stupidities, which cancelled each other out, until they produced the public will. The most insane thing of all was that the public will generally was the best choice.

Remo returned the girl's smile and she turned away with a shout. "Charlie," she called. "Get those brochures down into the truck."

"What truck?" a much whiskered young man said.

"On the side driveway. A green panel. It's taking the brochures to our other clubs around town."

"All right," Charlie said. He moved toward a half dozen bulky cartons of brochures that were on a four-wheeled hand truck. Remo walked over to give him a hand. He helped Charlie steer the car to the service elevator, then rode down with him, and helped Charlie load the brochures on the back of a green truck. They had just finished when the driver walked out of a saloon across the alley.

"You know where this stuff goes?" Charlie asked him.

"Got the list right here, kid," the driver said, patting his shirt pocket.

Charlie nodded and went back toward the hotel.

"I'll ride with you," Remo told the driver. "Help unload."

"Suit yourself."

The driver was humming "Sunshine is Nicer" all along the way. He turned on the radio and in Polaney's clear, resonant voice, they heard the same song on a commercial.

Two miles down the strip, the driver turned off Collins Avenue and began heading for the clubhouse in the northernmost section of Miami Beach. After a few blocks, the traffic thinned out to an occasional car.

"You for Cartwright?" Remo asked the driver, still humming the Polaney jingle.

"I voted for him last time," the driver said, in what Remo realized was a non-answer.

"Hey, wait a minute," Remo said. "Pull over here."

"What's the matter?"

"Just pull over. I've got to check the load."

The driver shrugged and pulled the truck to the side of a small roadway bridge that crossed a slimly built river. He stopped and turned to look at Remo who put him out with a knuckle to the neck.

The driver crumpled forward over the wheel. He would be out for a few minutes.

Remo hopped down from the truck and opened the side door in the little truck. Shielded from the highway by the body of the truck, he began to remove the cartons.

One at a time, he drove his steelhard fingertips into the boxes of brochures, perforating them with big jagged holes. Then, one at a time, he tossed them over the railing and into the water below. The holes would let the water flow in and destroy the printing.

Remo stuck a fifty dollar bill into the driver's shirt pocket, left him sleeping, went across the road and hitched a ride back into town.

So much for political counterespionage. Tonight, he thought, he might get a garden rake and go tear down the Cartwright billboards which were beginning to blossom around the city.

But first there was Farger.

Willard Farger, fourth deputy-assistant commissioner of elections, finally came to Remo. He came in a box, addressed simply "Remo" and delivered to the Polaney campaign headquarters. He came with an ice pick jammed into his right ear.

Remo looked down at Farger's body, scrunched up into the reinforced carton. A faint scent rose to his nostrils and he leaned forward, his face close to the box. He had smelled it before. It was floral. Yes. The same scent had come from the ice pick that he had seen jammed into the right ear of City Manager Moskowitz. It was lilac. A lilac-scented icepick.

Remo just looked at the ice pick in disgust. On its point had been skewered, not only Farger but the entire Polaney campaign. The only person in the whole campaign who knew anything at all, and he was dead.

It was the ultimate insanity, Remo thought. CURE, which had been created to use violence to help save the nation and its political processes, was now being destroyed by the most basic of the political processes—a free election—in which its opponents were free to use violence while Remo wasn't.

And he just did not know what to do about it.

For a moment, he thought of the phone. Smith was only a telephone call away. His hand began to move for the phone and then he shook his head, and began to lug the carton containing Farger's body to one of the back rooms.

CHAPTER TWENTY-TWO

After Remo had disposed of the body, he told of Farger's death to Teri Walker, who broke down and wept real tears.

"I didn't know politics was going to be like this," she cried. "That poor man."

"Well, we're not going to say a word about it," Remo said. "We're just going to go on campaigning."

She nodded and wiped her very wet eyes. "That's right. We've got to go on. He would have wanted us to."

"That's right," Remo said. "You go on. Do your commercials and your advertising. Do your thing."

"And you?"

"I'm going to do mine."

"We've got that television special Monday night," she said. "That might just win it for us."

"Good," Remo said. "The opposition's going to know they've been in a fight anyway."

Poor Teri. Her first campaign, and she was raising exuberance to an art form. But no matter what she did, there was no way to win. Remo conceded that now. There were no workers. And even if there had been workers, there was no work for them to do. Farger had kept everything in his head. Without him, Remo could not find the printing, the brochures, the bumper strips, the buttons, all the necessary paraphernalia of a political campaign.

He confided this to Chiun back at their hotel room.

"I do not understand," Chiun said. "You mean that people vote for one person, rather than another, because they prefer his button?"

"Well . . . sort of," Remo said.

"But you told me earlier that people would vote the way that police lieutenant told them to," Chiun said.

"Well . . . some people will."

"How can you tell the people who follow the police lieutenant from the people who follow the buttons?" Chiun asked.

"You can't," Remo said.

Chiun spattered the room with Korean, of which Remo could recognize a phrase or two, most dealing with the stupidity of democracy and how it was, therefore, the only form of government which white men deserved.

Finally, Chiun stopped. In English, he said: "What do you do now?"

"We can't win. But I can make things uncomfortable for them."

"But you told me that you could not kill your opponents."

"That's right. I can't. But I can rough them up a little, them and their campaign."

Chiun shook his head sadly. "An assassin who is not permitted to kill is like a man with an unloaded revolver who takes solace in the fact that at least the gun has a trigger. The risks are very great."

"But what else can I do? No workers, no equipment, no nothing," Remo said. "Let's face it, Chiun. The political campaign is over for us. We've lost."

"I see," Chiun said and watched as Remo changed into dark slacks and shirt and shoes.

"And now?" Chiun asked.

"I'm going to drop a little rainfall in the lives of our opposition."

"Do not be caught," Chiun said. "Because if you are, I will tell investigators everything I know. I understand it is the way of your country."

"Feel free," Remo said. "I won't be caught."

Remo got to the hotel headquarters of Mayor Tim Cartwright's campaign shortly after midnight. He left shortly before dawn, seen only by one person, and that only fleetingly, as that person decided it would be good to sleep until noon.

Behind him, Remo left a record of accomplishment, on which he would have been glad to campaign for a second term as campaign burglar.

He ripped out the telephone connections and rewired the junction boxes, until they were tangled mazes of colored cables. The telephone instruments themselves were carefully taken apart, their innards mangled, and then reinserted. Remo took apart the electric typewriters and re-jiggered the connections so that when struck, different keys produced the wrong letters. For good measure, he also bent the typewriter rollers.

He tore thousands of bumper strips in half. Thousands of copies of a campaign newsletter were dumped down the incinerator shaft, followed by three crates of lapel buttons. He painted mustache and beard on printed pictures of Mayor Cartwright, and as his last act, dropped a match down the incinerator shaft and waited for the flame to start with a muffled puff.

Remo decided to walk back to his hotel and he stopped in the early morning warmth and swam in the ocean. He swam strongly, powerfully slipping through the water in the way of Sinanju, his mind churning in marked contrast to the smooth moving of his body, and when his anger had waned and he turned in the water, the shoreline was out of sight. He had swum miles out to sea.

Slowly he returned to land, padding ashore in his briefs, then sitting in the sand and slipping on his clothes, under the startled eye of a beach boy who was setting up the chaise lounges for the day's invasion of freckled, pale-skinned New Yorkers.

He got back to his apartment by mid-morning. Chiun

should be up, he thought, and stuck his head into the old man's room. The cocoa mat on which Chiun sometimes slept was rolled up and neatly stored in a corner. The room was empty.

On the kitchen table, Remo found a note.

"A matter of urgency has taken me to Mr. Polaney's headquarters."

Now what? Remo decided he had better go and see.

Outside Polaney headquarters, the noise in the hall was deafening. What the hell was going on inside, Remo thought. Perhaps one of Farger's bunnies had lost her nail polish.

He pushed open the door to step inside, then stopped in amazement.

The place was overrun with people. Women. Middle-aged and elderly women. All moving, all working.

At Farger's desk sat Mrs. Ethel Hirshberg. She was shouting into a telephone.

"I don't know nothing from labor problems. You want to get paid, you deliver in an hour. Otherwise, you and your lovely family can eat the paper you used.

"That's right. One hour or no cash. Don't tell me about arrangements. This operation is under new management. That's right. One hour. And be sure you have somebody carry them upstairs. Us ladies have bad backs."

She hung up the phone and pointed to Remo. "Your father's inside. Now don't just stand there. Go inside and see if there's anything you can do to help, even though you're not much good for anything.

"Rose," she screamed. "You have that list of North Ward volunteers yet? Well, step on it. Get this show on the road." She turned to Remo again. "Hard," she said derisively. "After 40 years in the fur business, I'll teach you hard. Hard like you don't know hard. Why are you standing there? Report in to your father and see what it is you can do to help him. Poor old man. You should be ashamed of yourself, leaving this job to him until the last minute. And him so upset and all, for fear you might get hurt. And nice Mr. Polaney, that he shouldn't be stuck with someone like you."

Her phone rang and she picked it up before the first brrrrng had ended. "Sunshine is Nicer headquarters," she said, listened a moment, then barked, "I don't care what you promised, you're going to have those sound trucks here in one hour. One hour. That's right. Oh, no? Now listen. Do you know Judge Mandelbaum? Yes, well, he would be very interested to know that you are not willing to rent your trucks to anybody who calls. Did you know that's a violation of the federal fair election laws?" She shrugged at Remo. "Yes, that's right, and Judge Mandelbaum knows it, who is the husband of my cousin, Pearl. And anytime you shouldn't think that blood is thicker. . . ." She put her hand over the phone and shook her head at Remo again. "Inside," she hissed. "Help your father." Then she was back on the phone.

Remo shook his head in astonishment. There were fifty women working in the office, and more arriving each minute, brushing by Remo with a brusque "Unblock the door," tossing floppy flowered hats on tables, and without being directed, sitting down at desks and tables to begin working on what apparently were voter registration lists.

Mrs. Hirshberg hung up. "I got rid of your three playboy bunnies," she told Remo. "For campaign work, they are like zero. Maybe after the election, we find a nice place for them in a massage parlor somewhere."

Remo finally left the doorway and walked to the back office where Teri Walker usually worked. Inside, Chiun was seated behind her desk. He smiled when he looked up and saw Remo.

"My son," he said in greeting.

"My father," said Remo, bowing deferentially. "My resourceful, astonishing, devious, worry-about-me sneak of a father."

"Just so you shouldn't be forgetting," Chiun said.

CHAPTER TWENTY-THREE

By noon, three hundred women were on the streets of the city. They went door to door with literature. They assaulted the shopping centers. They broke into song at random moments:

"Sunshine is nicer.

"Vote for Polaney."

People who refused literature or who made nasty comments about Mac Polaney were subjected to cajolery. The easy abuse with which they dealt with each other had been left in campaign headquarters. On the street, under Mrs. Hirshberg's guidance, it was all sugar. "So, it wouldn't hurt you to vote for Mr. Polaney. So what's wrong with having a nice guy as mayor for a change. Look, I know how you feel, being Mayor Cartwright's sister and all, but why not be giving an honest man a chance. You can trust Mr. Polaney."

This was underway in full force at 12 noon. At 12:01 P.M., the Cartwright headquarters were aware of what was happening. At 12:35 P.M., countermeasures were underway.

It would be very simple, Marshal Dworshansky explained to Cartwright. These are volunteers who therefore have no real stake in Tuesday's election. Make an object lesson of one or two of them and the others will quickly find very good reasons to return to their Mah Jongg games.

This was subsequently explained to Theophilus Pedaster and Gumbo Jackson, who were assigned by a friend of theirs to deliver this object lesson.

"Women, you say?" said Theophilus Pedaster, giggling. "Young women or old women?"

"Old women."

Pedaster looked disappointed. Gumbo Jackson, however, did not. He was the smarter of the two and had already taken the four hundred dollars offered for the job and placed it in his pocket. "Young women, old women," he said, "it doesn't matter. Just a leeetle lesson." And he grinned because it had all been carefully explained to him.

Unforunately, someone had forgotten to explain it nearly that carefully to a little old Oriental in orange robes, who was accompanying the first group of ladies that Pedaster and Jackson confronted.

"Give us all them leaflets," Pedaster had said.

"You get one each," said the big-busted woman in the blue dress, who was leading the group.

"Ah wants them all," Pedaster repeated.

"You get one."

Pedaster pulled a knife from his pocket. "You don't understand. Ah needs them all." He looked at Gumbo Jackson who also pulled a knife.

"Protect Chiun," the bosomy woman yelled, and then swung her purse up over her head, down onto Pedaster's skull. Three women joined her, swinging their heavy pocketbooks. It was bad, man, and finally Pedaster decided he better cut somebody.

But that didn't work either. In the mix of bodies and arms and pocketbooks, he saw an orange-robed arm flash, and his knife was gone. Worse yet, his arm was disabled. He turned toward Gumbo, just in time to see an orange flash bury deep into Gumbo's stomach. Gumbo splatted onto the sidewalk like a fresh egg.

Pedaster looked at his lifelong closest friend there, unconscious on the ground, the women hovering over him, and he did what he had been trained to do since childhood. He fled.

Behind him, he heard the women babbling: "Is Chiun all right? Are you okay? These shvartzes didn't hurt you?"

It was only when he got three blocks away that Pedaster realized Gumbo had the four hundred. Oh well, let him keep it. If he lived, he deserved it. Pedaster would have no need for it, since he was going to visit his family in Alabama. Right away.

By nightfall, every hand in the city had held a piece of Polaney Literature. The next day, every house was visisted by a team of women who explained why all decent, self-respecting persons would vote only for Polaney. There were so many Polaney volunteers on the street that Cartwright workers began to feel oppressed, skulking across streets, ducking into bars, chucking their remaining literature down sewers rather than risk the wrath of the sharp-tongued women who somehow had gotten onto Polaney's bandwagon.

And over the entire city rang the noise of the sound trucks:

"Sunshine is Nicer.

"Vote for Polaney."

In the taverns and the living rooms, whose air conditioning sealed out the sound truck noises from the street, the message came pouring out of televisions and radios, saturating Miami Beach.

Vote for Polaney.

The message even found its way onto a cabin radio in a large white and silvered yacht, bobbing gently a half mile off the shore of the city.

Marshal Dworshansky angrily flipped the radio off, and turned to his daughter, immaculate and cool in a white linen pants suit.

"I had not expected this," Dworshansky said, beginning to pace, his heavily muscled arms bulging under a tight blue tee shirt.

"What?"

"That Polaney would be able to put together such a campaign. I had not expected," he said reproachfully, "that your work for him would be quite so productive."

"I don't understand it," said Dorothy Walker. "I personally approved the commercials and the advertising because they were the worst I had ever seen. The best way for them to waste their money."

"Waste money? Hah," said the old man who, at that moment, looked old and mean. "That money might buy the election. We must find something else."

Dorothy Walker stood up and smoothed the front of her pants-suit jacket. "Father," she said, "it is a thing I think I must do for you. We will find if this Remo has a weak spot."

CHAPTER TWENTY-FOUR

"I want a hundred in a package," Mrs. Ethel Hirshberg told Remo. "Not ninety-nine. Not one hundred one. I want one hundred. So count them."

"You count them," Remo said. "There's one hundred in these packages."

"How can there be one hundred when you don't count them? Just reach in and grab, pull out anything and tell me it's one hundred? I shouldn't be like you in business, thank heavens."

"It's one hundred," said Remo stubbornly. Ethel Hirshberg had had him at the job for over an hour now, breaking down vast boxes of brochures into stacks of 100 for wrapping and distribution to volunteers. Remo did it like a card trick, running his fingers down the side of a stack until he knew there were 100 brochures there. "It's one hundred," he repeated.

"But you count," Ethel Hirshberg said.

Chiun came out of Teri Walker's office. He was wearing his heavy black brocaded robe and his serenity was like a force of nature.

"Chiun," Remo yelled.

Chiun turned, looked at Remo without expression, and then smiled as his face came to rest on Mrs. Hirshberg.

"Come here, will you," said Remo.

Mrs. Hirshberg shook her head. "Your father. Your father, yet, and you talk like that. Come here. No respect at all for your elders. Or your betters."

Chiun approached them.

Remo and Ethel both tried to state their own case first.

"I want piles of one hundred. . . ."

"These are piles of one hundred. . . ."

"So it shouldn't hurt to count them. Just to make sure we don't waste them. . . ."

"I don't have to count them if I know there's a hundred here."

Chiun raised a hand on Remo's dying words: "How many are in this pile, Chiun?"

Chiun looked at the pile of leaflets in front of Remo, lifted it into his hand, and said magisterially, "This pile contains 102 brochures."

"See," Ethel said. "Count them from now on." She walked away, and Remo said, "Chiun, why did you say that? You know there's only one hundred in that pile."

"You are so sure? The infallible one cannot make a mistake?"

"No, I can make a mistake, but I didn't. There's one hundred here."

"So? For two brochures, you argue with volunteer labor? Does one win war by losing all battles?"

"Dammit, Chiun, I can't let that woman browbeat me any more. I've been working here forever. One hundred is one hundred. Why should I count them when I can finger-weigh them?"

"Because if you do not count them, all our ladies will walk out the door. Then what will you do? Go back to foolish child's plan of partial violence against the enemy? A plan that will most likely destroy you? And your Mr. Polaney? Does he just go back, quietly, to losing?"

"Chiun, I liked it better when we were losing."

"Losers always like it better when losing. The act of winning takes not only discipline but morality."

"The morality of saying one hundred is really one hundred and two?" Remo asked.

"The morality of saying it is two hundred and fourteen if that is necessary."

"Chiun, you are despicable."

"You are sloppy and that is worse. While this pack does contain one hundred, that one contains only ninety-nine."

He pointed to another stack of brochures, seven feet away on the long table.

"Wrong, Chiun. One hundred."

"Ninety-nine,"

"You'll see," Remo said. He leaned over, snatched up the suspect pile, and began to count them loudly onto the table. "One. Two. Three."

As he counted, Chiun walked away, back toward Mrs. Hirshberg's desk.

"He understands now," Chiun said gently. "You see, he is not really bad. Just lazy."

Over the room came Remo's voice.

"Seventeen.

"Eighteen.

"Nineteen."

"Like so many young people today," Ethel Hirshberg said, consoling Chiun. "I never thought to ask. Can he count to one hundred?"

"He need only reach ninety nine with that pile," Chiun said.

"Twenty-five.

"Twenty-six.

"Twenty-seven."

Dorothy Walker seemed to exude cool breezes as she came through the door, crisp and fresh in a white suit, and paused at Mrs. Hirshberg's desk.

"Is Remo in?" she said.

Ethel Hirshberg raised a finger to her lips. "Shhh," she said. "He is busy right now."

"Forty-seven.

"Forty-eight.

"Forty-nine."

"Will he be done soon?" Dorothy Walker said, looking at Remo, whose head was down over the table in intense concentration.

"He's only got fifty more to count," Mrs. Hirshberg said. "For him, another fifteen minutes?"

"I'll wait."

"Please do."

"Sixty-four.

"Sixty-five.

"Sixty-six."

As Dorothy Walker waited, her eyes roamed the headquarters, quietly impressed by the efficiency and organization with which more than two dozen volunteers were carrying out logistical work.

"Ninety-seven.

"Ninety-eight.

"Ninety-nine.

"NINETY-NINE?"

Remo looked up and saw Dorothy Walker. He smiled toward her and approached.

"Yes?" Chiun said.

"Yes, what?"

"You have nothing to say?"

"What's to say?"

"There were how many?" Chiun asked.

"I don't know," Remo said.

"You don't know?"

"I don't know. I got tired and stopped counting at ninety-nine."

Of the next words, Remo recognized a few. He would ignore Chiun. Remo, at least, would not stoop to petty bickering.

Dorothy Walker smiled at him. "I thought I'd see how the winner lives," she said.

"You think so?" Remo said.

"You can't miss."

"Just so long as Albert Einstein here doesn't count the votes," Mrs. Hirshberg interrupted.

"Come on," Remo said to Dorothy Walker. "These lower-echelon types don't understand us creative people."

"Is Teri around?"

"She said everything was in the can for tomorrow's commercials and advertisements. She was going out of town to stay with a friend, and she said she'd see us tomorrow night at the TV studio," Remo said.

Dorothy Walker nodded. "I'll talk to her tomorrow," she said.

She let Remo lead her out. He enjoyed it. She looked good and smelled even nicer—a fresh, crisp floral scent.

The scent was even stronger in his nostrils later, in Dorothy Walker's apartment, when she took from his hand the glass she had put there, pressed her body against his and planted her mouth on his.

She stayed locked there a long time, exuding her clean aroma into Remo's nostrils. He watched a tiny pulse in her temple increase its speed.

She stopped, and led Remo by the hand out onto the balcony of the penthouse. Up here, above the lights of the strip, the night was black. She still held Remo's hand as, with her other hand, she stretched out far to the left and then swept around past the sea in front of them, then further on, until her hand swung in front of Remo and came up onto his shoulder. She leaned her head against his upper arm.

"Remo, this could all be ours," she said.

"Ours?"

"I've decided that my firm is going to open a political division, and I want you to head it."

Remo, who knew that he had obvious political skills and was pleased that they were recognized, paused a moment, then said, "Sorry. That's not my line."

"Just what is your line?"

"I like to move from place to place, doing good wherever I go," he said, feeling for a moment that it was true, and sensing the satisfaction the same lie always gave Chiun.

"Let's not fool each other, Remo," she said. "I know you feel the same attraction for me that I do for you. Now how can we be together? To satisfy that attraction? How and where and when?"

To which Remo replied, "How about here and now? Like this."

He had her there, on the smooth tile of the balcony, their own body smells mingling and strengthening the cool flowered smell of Dorothy Walker. To Remo, it was a gift, a parting gift. She would go on to become a political manager; Remo, he knew, would go back to doing what he did—being the second-best assassin in the world. It would have been heartless of him, not to give her some way to remember him in those empty years she faced ahead.

So he gave of himself, until she shuddered and lay, smiling still, beneath him.

And later, she said, "This is a dirty business, this politics, Remo. Let's forget Polaney. Let's go now."

Remo watched the stars blink in the blackness overhead and said, "Too late now. There's no turning back."

"Just an election?" she asked.

He shook his head. "Not just an election. First, I elect Polaney. And then I do what I really came to do."

"It's that important?" she said. "This thing that you do?"

"I don't know whether it's important or not," he said. "But it's what I do, and so I do it. I guess it's important."

And then he had her again.

When the door clicked shut behind him, Dorothy Walker rose and went to the telephone. Her number came through quickly.

"Papa," she said. "This Remo *is* your government man, and I don't think there's any way to make him back off. He believes in what he's doing."

Then: "Yes, Papa, I suppose there is always that way. It's just truly a shame. He is a man like you, papa."

CHAPTER TWENTY-FIVE

"For my next number, I would like to play Nola. I would also like to play the Flight of the Bumblebee. Since I can't play either of them, I'll try to play My Old Kentucky Home."

Mac Polaney was wearing frayed bottom shorts, sneakers with no socks, a red boatneck shirt, and a baseball cap with a script B on it that looked like an old Brooklyn Dodger issue.

He sat on a wooden stool, braced his long woodcutting saw against one foot, and began to stroke it with a violin bow. The wailing theramin sound it made was a reasonable facsimile of My Old Kentucky Home.

In the wings Remo winced.

"This is terrible," he hissed to Chiun. "Where's Teri?"

"Her whereabouts are not my campaign assignment," Chiun said. "Besides, I think he plays his strange instrument extremely well. It is an art alien to my homeland."

"And to mine," Remo said. "We must be losing hundreds of votes a minute."

"One can never tell," Chiun said. "Perhaps Miami Beach is ready for a saw virtuoso in City Hall. He may be an idea whose time has come."

"Thank you, Chiun, for consoling me."

Remo and Chiun watched in silence as Mac Polaney hammed it up for the television camera. But where was Teri Walker? She was supposed to have been there.

Perhaps, she could have gotten Mac Polaney to talk about the campaign a little. Particularly with what this three-hour extravaganza was costing Remo. And she certainly would have known how to handle that out-of-town television crew. They had told studio people and Remo that they were from a New York-based network and were filming a special on election techniques. After some haggling, they were allowed to set up their camera in the opposite wing of the stage, and now the two men manning it kept it fixed on Polaney running off miles of film. They made Remo uneasy, but he chalked it off to his long-standing feeling that disasters should be kept in the family and not filmed for posterity.

Chiun was saying something to him.

"Shhhh," said Remo. "I want to see if he reaches the high note."

Polaney almost reached it. Chiun insisted, "There are other vibrations you might consider."

"Such as?"

"Such as those two gentlemen of television over there. They are not authentic."

"Why?"

"Because for the last five minutes, their picture machine has been aimed at that stain on the ceiling."

Remo looked. Sure enough, the camera was pointing away from Polaney, its film grinding rapidly away. The two cameramen were kneeling down next to their equipment box. As Remo and Chiun watched, they came up standing, guns in their hands, focused on Polaney.

All the people out there in what Mac Polaney had called "television land" missed the most exciting part of his campaign special. Remo moved for the gunmen, but Chiun was already there. Viewers had seen only a green swish as the robed Chiun moved across the stage, past Polaney, and then, as Polaney finished his number with one last dying note, they heard shots, then sharp thwacks, then screams.

The cameraman surrendered to his instinct and turned the camera off Polaney and swung it to the side. Chiun hopped nimbly back behind the drapes and the camera saw only the bodies of the two bogus cameramen, lying there on the bare wooden floor, unmoving, dead.

The camera froze there a moment, then began moving back to Polaney. With horror, Remo realized he was standing directly between Polaney and the camera, ready to present his face to the audience for posterity and all he could think of was how Dr. Smith would resent it. Remo turned his back to the camera and said into the overhead microphone:

"Do not be alarmed, ladies and gentlemen. An attempt has just been made on Mr. Polaney's life, but our security guards have the situation well in hand."

Then, still without turning, without showing his face to the camera, Remo sidled off the stage, leaving framed in the center of the camera lens Mac Polaney, holding his saw by the handle, looking off toward the side of the stage where the dead men lay.

Finally Polaney turned back toward the camera.

Slowly he said:

"They were trying to silence me. But people have tried to silence me before, and they all have failed. Because only death would silence me."

He stopped. A cameraman cheered. In the control booth, an engineer applauded.

Polaney waited a moment, then said: "I hope you will all vote for me tomorrow. Good night."

And with his saw under his arm, he moved away, off camera, into the wings where Remo stood, now joined by Chiun. The music of "Sunshine is Nicer" came up and over.

"That was quick thinking," Remo said.

"Quick thinking? About what?" Polaney asked.

"That bit about people trying to silence you. Real good politics."

"But it's true," Polaney said. "Every time I play the saw, someone's trying to keep me quiet."

"You were talking about the saw?"

"Well, of course. What else?"

"Where's Teri?" Remo bawled.

Teri Walker was not in the small apartment she kept in the hotel which housed Polaney's campaign headquarters, but something else was.

On her desk, Remo found a note. It read: "Teri. Under no circumstances, go to the studio tonight. This is important. Mother." The note was fresh and fragrant and Remo lifted it to his face. It even smelled like Dorothy Walker. It had that clean . . . and then he realized it. It had the smell of lilacs. The same smell that had been on the ice picks he had found in Willard Farger and City Manager Clyde Moskowitz.

Dorothy Walker. She had been the leak from the Polaney campaign, taking Remo's money and playing both sides against the middle. And the night before, she had tried to use him.

Remo walked to Dorothy Walker's nearby penthouse apartment, forced the door, and sat on the soft brown arm chair in the living room and waited. He waited through the night and until the sun was high. No Dorothy Walker. And finally the phone rang.

Remo picked it up.

"Hello."

"Hello, who's this? Remo?" said Teri Walker.

"Right."

She giggled. "So my mother finally trapped you. I knew she would."

"Afraid not, Teri. Your mom's not here. She hasn't been here all night."

"Oh. She must be out on Grandpa's boat. Probably talking about the campaign. He's very interested."

"What boat?" Remo said.

"The Encolpius," she said. "It's tied up in the bay."

"Thanks," Remo said. "By the way, why didn't you show up at the studio last night?"

"Momma left me a note and told me not to. When I talked to her on the phone, she said there was a chance of violence, and that you said it was best I stayed away. So I stayed at my friend's house again. But I watched. I thought it was wonderful."

"If you think that was good, watch what comes next," Remo said.

He hung up and left the apartment building, walking toward the water.

"You've lost, poppa," Dorothy Walker was wearing a green cocktail dress in the main sittingroom of the yacht, talking to Marshal Dworshansky.

"I know, my dear. I know. But who would have thought our men would miss? And such good men. Sasha and Dmitri. They would have done anything for us."

"Yes, but miss they did. And now there is no way that Mr. Polaney is not going to win the election. You failed to consider the public reaction if your men missed."

"That is true." Dworshansky smiled sadly. "Perhaps I am just growing old. Too old to have my own city. Well. There are other fish in the sea."

"Maybe now, papa, you'll retire as you should have years ago. Losing, you always told me, is the only sin."

"Do I detect a note of exultation? You may have lost something too," he said.

"No, papa, I've won. Polaney will be the mayor. Teri and I will be his closest advisors. Inside of six months, I will own the city. And then I will give it to you. I owe you that gift."

As Dworshansky listened, he understood that Dorothy Walker's offer of a gift was not made in love, but as full payment of an annoying debt. He looked at her and said, "Perhaps we both have lost something."

"That's right," came a voice. Remo stood in the doorway. "You've both lost."

"Who are you?" Dworshansky demanded. "Who is this man?"

Dorothy stood up and smiled at Remo. "This is Remo, my associate from Mr. Polaney's campaign. The only other person with enough vision to see that Mac Polaney was what Miami Beach needed."

"Save it for your next dog food commercial," Remo said. "I finally wised up. When I found out why Teri wasn't at the studio. Did you do it just to capture the city?"

Dworshansky nodded. "Why not?" he said. "Can you think of a better reason?" He talked easily, almost happily.

"But why kill Farger?"

"Farger? Oh yes. That was just to remind Mayor Cartwright's people that we did not look kindly upon defections. Of course, when you disposed of Farger's body and kept the killing quiet, that eliminated any value we might have gotten from it."

"And Moskowitz?"

"Moskowitz was weak," Dworshansky said. "I think he would rather have gone to jail than to play in this high-stakes game. We could not chance somebody on the inside cracking."

"And you dragged the federal government and the League papers into the campaign because. . . ."

". . . . Because it was the only way to keep Cartwright and his thieves out of jail and to get Cartwright reelected. You see, I figured that the government would be afraid to act against Cartwright if it was, itself, under fire from him."

"Good plan," Remo said. "It tied my hands for a long time, made me afraid to do what should have been done to Cartwright and to you. Too bad you finally lost."

Dworshansky smiled. A deep white smile in his dark tan face. "No, my friend. I have not lost. You have lost."

He lunged for a small box on top of the sitting room's piano and answered Remo's last question.

When he drew out the ice pick, Remo realized that he —not Cartwright, not Dorothy Walker, not any of the hired hands—this muscled old man had been the killer. He had wanted to clear that up.

Remo grinned.

Dworshansky charged him. As he got close to Remo, Remo could smell the overpowering aroma of the lilac cologne. Dworshansky wasted no time on preliminaries. He aimed a roundhouse at Remo's temple, hoping to drive the ice pick in to the hilt. Remo slid back, just out of the pick's range, then moved forward again, slamming the hell out of his left hand against Dworshansky's right arm, forcing the pick to continue its giant arc, until it buried itself deep into the left side of Dworshansky's own throat. The man gurgled, looked at Remo in shock and surprise, then dropped to the floor.

Dorothy Walker stood. She cast only a fleeting glance at her father, then said: "Oh, Remo. We can do it. You and I. First this city and then the state."

"Not even one tear to shed for your father?"

She moved close to Remo, insinuating her body against his. She smiled. "Not even one," she said. "I've always been too busy living . . . and loving . . . to weep."

"We'll see what we can do to correct that," Remo said. Before she could move or react, her scream was frozen in her throat as Remo calmly shattered her temple. He let her down softly on the floor, next to her father, and closed the sitting room door behind him.

Remo found the yacht empty of crew. He moved the big boat down to the southern tip of Miami Beach and anchored it two hundred yards off shore. The crew, who had been given the afternoon off by Dworshansky, was not likely to happen upon it there. Remo swam into the beach. The next stop on his schedule was Mayor Tim Cartwright.

CHAPTER TWENTY-SIX

Mayor Timothy Cartwright opened his upper right desk drawer. Where there would be an opening on a normal desk, here there was a metal slide. Cartwright unclipped his keychain from the back of his belt, and with a thin steel key unlocked the slide.

He took from the drawer piles of bills, twenties, fifties, hundreds and shoveled them into his briefcase.

How many times, he thought, had losing candidates delayed their appearance before their supporters at campaign headquarters? And how many times had they been too busy to speak, because they had first had to go to their offices to collect the money and get rid of the evidence?

Well, it didn't matter. He had come in honest and poor; he would go out dishonest and rich. The money in safe deposit boxes around the country; the jewelry and bonds overseas. He would never have to worry about the future. The city had chosen Mac Polaney, so that was their problem. Let the voters live with it. He would be far away.

And when police protection fell apart, when city services became first negligible, then non-existent, when the town was an open city for hoodlums, bums and hippies, and the public clamored for Tim Cartwright to come back and straighten things out, they could hold their hands on their asses. He would be long gone.

He visualized his headquarters now, awash with tears. How strange. There were more tears shed by one rabid supporter than by all the losing incumbents in the history of the world. Not strange at all, he then realized. The losing incumbent had already gotten his; what did he have to cry about?

"Going somewhere?"

The voice broke Cartwright's reverie.

"How did you get in here?" he said, knowing that the building was locked and Sheriff Clyde McAdow stood guard at the back entrance of the municipal building.

"The sheriff decided to take a nap. A long nap. Now it's your turn."

"You're that Remo, aren't you?" Cartwright said. His hand moved stealthily toward a desk drawer.

"That's right," Remo said. "And if your hand reaches that drawer, your hand'll come off."

Cartwright froze, then said casually, "Why? What have you got against me?"

"A few things. Farger. Moskowitz. The attempt on Polaney?"

"You know they were all the marshal's idea, don't you?" Cartwright said. "Not mine. His."

"I know," Remo said. "Everything was his idea. The League papers. Killing poor Bullingsworth. Attacking Folcroft. The federal government."

Cartwright shrugged his shoulders and grinned, the kind of grin mastered best by Irish politicians caught with their hands in the till.

"So? It was true, wasn't it? You're here."

"That's right," Remo said. "We're both here."

"Now what?"

"Here's what. You sit down at that desk and write what I dictate."

Cartwright nodded. "Okay. That's what you get out of it. What do I get out of it?"

"You live. That's one. That briefcase of money. That's two. A free ride out of the country. That's three."

"Do you mind if I call the marshal?"

"Yes," Remo said, "I do mind. He told me he would not accept your call."

Cartwright measured Remo again with his eyes, then with an almost imperceptible shrug, sat down at the desk, took Mayor's Office stationery from the center drawer and a pen from the ebony desk set in front of him. He looked up at Remo.

"Address it," Remo said, "to the people of Miami Beach."

Mac Polaney held the paper up in his hands.

To celebrate his new found eminence as mayor-elect of Miami Beach, he had dressed in a pair of full length blue jeans. His white tennis sneakers had given way to open toed leather thong sandals. In place of a red boat-neck shirt, he was wearing a long sleeved pink silk shirt with Catfish Corners Bowling Team embroidered on the back.

"Copies of this paper are being made ready for you members of the press," he said. "In it, Mayor Cartwright tells how he tried to confuse the citizenry about the League papers. They were all a fraud, he said. The only purpose was to draw attention away from his shakedowns and extortion, which he freely admits to in the letter.

"He apologizes to the people of Miami Beach and as the next mayor, I accept the apology for the people of Miami Beach and cordially invite soon-to-be former Mayor Cartwright to the annual Catfish-in-June festival, which will award a hundred dollar prize for the catch of the largest catfish, even if I warn him not to think about winning the money, because I am going to be entered and will probably win. In addition, according to Mayor Cartwright's statement which I have here in my hand, he doesn't need an extra hundred dollars. He's got enough money."

"Where is the mayor now?" one reporter asked.

Mac Polaney wiped his brow in the heat of the overhead TV lights. "You're looking at him, bub."

"To what do you attribute your landslide victory?"

"To clean living and eight hundred international units of Vitamin E each and every day."

Remo turned from the television set. "All right, let's go," he said. He pushed Cartwright out of the dingy waterfront bar and led him to the end of the dock where they boarded a small outboard motor boat. In two minutes, Remo was at the Encolpius, following Cartwright up the gangplank to the main deck. Cartwright still clutched his money-filled attache case.

"Where is the marshal?" Cartwright asked.

"Right in here," Remo said, pushing open the door to the main sitting room. Cartwright walked past Remo, saw on the floor the bodies of Dworshansky and his daughter, and turned back to Remo. "You promised," he said.

"Never trust a politician's promise," Remo said, just before his hard, iron-edge hand crashed against Cartwright's skull. As Cartwright dropped, Remo said: "You peaked too early."

Remo moved to the bow of the boat, started the yacht's engines, and set the automatic pilot on a low-speed course heading due east. Then he went down below into the engine room, emptied out one of the diesel tanks, and spilled its contents all over the engine room. On top of that, for good measure, he emptied another twenty gallon drum of regular gasoline, setting a small trail of saturated rags and papers out into the passageway.

He dropped a match into the rags which lit with a puff, as Remo ran up the stairway to the main deck and slid down the steps into his motor boat which was being pulled along by the powerful yacht. He untied the ropes lashing him to the yacht, let his boat drift away for a hundred yards, then started his own motor and aimed the small outboard back to shore.

Halfway to the shore, he heard a loud thump behind

him. He turned around and saw a flash of fire. He cut his motor and watched. The flames burned brightly, slowly reduced themselves to a glow, and then exploded with a crashing thump that resounded in Remo's ears. Seconds later, the sea was again still.

Remo stared at the spot for awhile, then turned his attention and his boat back to shore.

Later that night, Remo watched the television news.

It was a tapestry of complicated story after complicated story. Reporters hinted that Mayor Cartwright had fled after submitting his confession to Polaney. They speculated that Cartwright himself had killed Bullingsworth and Moskowitz because they had unmasked his thefts, and then had killed Sheriff Clyde McAdow, whose body was found in the city hall parking lot, because McAdow had tried to prevent his escape.

And then of course there was Mac Polaney's overwhelming election victory, and the television film of his press conference, at which he announced his first appointment, Mrs. Ethel Hirshberg, as city treasurer.

Mrs. Hirshberg grabbed the microphone from him and said, "I vow to watch city money like it was mine and to keep an eye on the mayor and to treat him like my own son, for which I have plenty of time since my son never even calls me."

Remo could take no more. He flipped off the television and dialed the 800 area-code number.

It rang. Once. Twice. Three times. And then it was picked up.

"Yes?" said the lemony voice.

"Remo here."

"Yes," said Dr. Smith. "I recognize the voice. Even if it has been a long while."

"I've pulled your irons out of the fire," Remo said.

"Oh? I was not aware I had any irons in the fire."

"Have you seen the news? Polaney's election. Cartwright's confession that the League papers were all a fake."

"Yes, I've seen the news. I wonder where Mayor Cartwright has gone, by the way?"

"He's gone to sea," Remo said.

"I see," Smith said. "I will carry your report to Number One. He returns tonight, you know."

"I know," Remo said. "We political types keep on top of the news."

"Is that all?" Smith asked.

"I suppose so."

"Goodbye."

Smith hung up and Remo replaced the telephone, feeling disgusted. He looked at Chiun.

"Does one expect thanks from an emperor?" Chiun said.

"I wasn't expecting to have my feet kissed if that's what you mean. But maybe, just a thank you. Just saying it wouldn't have been hard."

"Emperors do not thank," Chiun said. "They pay for and expect the best. Just consider yourself blessed that you were almost the city treasurer of Miami Beach."

THE END

Warren Murphy

CELEBRATING 10 YEARS IN PRINT
AND OVER 20 MILLION COPIES SOLD!

☐ 41-216-9 Created, The Destroyer #1	$1.95	☐ 41-239-8 King's Curse #24	$1.95
☐ 41-217-7 Death Check #2	$1.95	☐ 40-901-X Sweet Dreams #25	$1.75
☐ 41-218-5 Chinese Puzzle #3	$1.95	☐ 40-902-8 In Enemy Hands #26	$1.75
☐ 41-219-3 Mafia Fix #4	$1.95	☐ 41-242-8 Last Temple #27	$1.95
☐ 41-220-7 Dr Quake #5	$1.95	☐ 41-243-6 Ship of Death #28	$1.95
☐ 41-221-5 Death Therapy #6	$1.95	☐ 40-905-2 Final Death #29	$1.75
☐ 41-222-3 Union Bust #7	$1.95	☐ 40-110-8 Mugger Blood #30	$1.50
☐ 40-884-6 Summit Chase #8	$1.75	☐ 40-907-9 Head Men #31	$1.75
☐ 41-224-X Murder's Shield #9	$1.95	☐ 40-908-7 Killer Chromosomes #32	$1.75
☐ 41-225-8 Terror Squad #10	$1.95	☐ 40-909-5 Voodoo Die #33	$1.75
☐ 41-226-6 Kill Or Cure #11	$1.95	☐ 41-249-5 Chained Reaction #34	**$1.95**
☐ 41-227-4 Slave Safari #12	$1.95	☐ 41-250-9 Last Call #35	$1.95
☐ 41-228-2 Acid Rock #13	$1.95	☐ 41-251-7 Power Play #36	$1.95
☐ 41-229-0 Judgment Day #14	$1.95	☐ 41-252-5 Bottom Line #37	$1.95
☐ 41-768-3 Murder Ward #15	$2.25	☐ 41-253-3 Bay City Blast #38	$1.95
☐ 41-231-2 Oil Slick #16	$1.95	☐ 41-254-1 Missing Link #39	$1.95
☐ 41-232-0 Last War Dance #17	$1.95	☐ 40-714-9 Dangerous Games #40	$1.75
☐ 40-894-3 Funny Money #18	$1.75	☐ 41-766-7 Firing Line #41	**$2.25**
☐ 40-895-1 Holy Terror #19	$1.75	☐ 41-767-5 Timber Line #42	**$2.25**
☐ 41-235-5 Assassins Play-Off #20	$1.95	☐ 40-717-3 Midnight Man #43	$1.95
☐ 41-236-3 Deadly Seeds #21	$1.95	☐ 40-718-1 Balance of Power #44	$1.95
☐ 40-898-6 Brain Drain #22	$1.75	☐ 40-719-X Spoils of War #45	$1.95
☐ 41-238-X Child's Play #23	$1.95	☐ 40-720-3 Next of Kin #46	$1.95

Canadian orders must be paid with U.S Bank check or U.S Postal money order only.

Buy them at your local bookstore or use this handy coupon

Clip and mail this page with your order

PINNACLE BOOKS, INC.—Reader Service Dept.
1430 Broadway, New York, NY 10018

Please send me the book(s) I have checked above. I am enclosing $_____ (please add 75¢ to cover postage and handling). Send check or money order only—no cash or C.O.D.'s.

Mr./Mrs./Miss _____

Address _____

City _____ State/Zip _____

Please allow six weeks for delivery. Prices subject to change without notice.

The Destroyer

FREE POSTER OFFER!

A full-color, 16 by 20 inch limited edition poster, reprinted from an original painting by Hector Garrido, can be yours—absolutely free—simply by sending your name and address, plus $2.50 to help defray the cost of postage and handling.

Clip and mail this page with your order

PINNACLE BOOKS, INC.— Reader Service Dept
1430 Broadway, New York, NY 10018

Please send me the free poster described above. I am enclosing $2.50 to cover postage and handling. Send check or money order only— no cash or C.O.D.'s.

Mr./Mrs./Miss _____

Address _____

City _____ State/Zip _____

Canadian orders must be paid with U.S. Bank check or U.S. Postal money order only.

Offer expires June 30, 1982. Void where prohibited by law.
Please allow 8 weeks for delivery.

the EXECUTIONER by Don Pendleton

Relax...and enjoy more of America's #1 bestselling action/adventure series! Over 25 million copies in print!

- ☐ 41-065-4 War Against The Mafia #1 $2.25
- ☐ 41-714-4 Death Squad #2 $2.25
- ☐ 41-669-7 Battle Mask #3 $2.25
- ☐ 41-068-9 Miami Massacre #4 $1.95
- ☐ 41-069-7 Continental Contract #5 $1.95
- ☐ 41-070-0 Assault On Soho #6 $1.95
- ☐ 41-071-9 Nightmare In New York #7 $1.95
- ☐ 41-763-2 Chicago Wipeout #8 $2.25
- ☐ 41-073-5 Vegas Vendetta #9 $1.95
- ☐ 41-074-3 Caribbean Kill #10 $1.95
- ☐ 41-075-1 California Hit #11 $1.95
- ☐ 41-076-X Boston Blitz #12 $1.95
- ☐ 41-077-8 Washington I.O.U. #13 $1.95
- ☐ 41-078-6 San Diego Siege #14 $1.95
- ☐ 41-079-4 Panic In Philly #15 $1.95
- ☐ 41-080-8 Sicilian Slaughter #16 $1.95
- ☐ 40-753-X Jersey Guns #17 $1.75
- ☐ 41-764-0 Texas Storm #18 $2.25
- ☐ 40-755-6 Detroit Deathwatch #19 $1.75
- ☐ 40-756-4 New Orleans Knockout #20 $1.75
- ☐ 40-757-2 Firebase Seattle #21 $1.75
- ☐ 41-086-7 Hawaiian Hellground #22 $1.95
- ☐ 40-759-9 St. Louis Showdown #23 $1.75
- ☐ 40-760-2 Canadian Crisis #24 $1.75
- ☐ 41-089-1 Colorado Kill-Zone #25 $1.95
- ☐ 41-090-5 Acapulco Rampage #26 $1.95
- ☐ 41-091-3 Dixie Convoy #27 $1.95
- ☐ 41-092-1 Savage Fire #28 $1.95
- ☐ 40-765-3 Command Strike #29 $1.75
- ☐ 41-094-8 Cleveland Pipeline #30 $1.95
- ☐ 41-095-6 Arizona Ambush #31 $1.95
- ☐ 41-096-4 Tennessee Smash #32 $1.95
- ☐ 41-097-2 Monday's Mob #33 $1.95
- ☐ 41-765-9 Terrible Tuesday #34 $2.25
- ☐ 41-099-9 Wednesday's Wrath #35 $1.95
- ☐ 41-100-6 Thermal Thursday #36 $1.95
- ☐ 41-101-4 Friday's Feast #37 $1.95
- ☐ 40-338-0 Satan's Sabbath #38 $1.75
- ☐ 41-700-4 Executioner Trilogy: The Beginning (trade size) $5.95

Canadian orders must be paid with U.S. Bank check or U.S. Postal money order only.

Buy them at your local bookstore or use this handy coupon

Clip and mail this page with your order

 PINNACLE BOOKS, INC.—Reader Service Dept.
1430 Broadway, New York, NY 10018

Please send me the book(s) I have checked above. I am enclosing $_____ (please add 75¢ to cover postage and handling). Send check or money order only—no cash or C.O.D.'s.

Mr./Mrs./Miss _____

Address _____

City _____ State/Zip _____

Please allow six weeks for delivery. Prices subject to change without notice.

by Lionel Derrick

More bestselling action/adventure from Pinnacle, America's #1 series publisher!

- ☐ 40-101-9 Target Is H #1 — $1.25
- ☐ 40-102-7 Blood on the Strip #2 — $1.25
- ☐ 40-423-9 Hijacking Manhattan #4 — $1.50
- ☐ 40-424-7 Mardi Gras Massacre #5 — $1.50
- ☐ 40-493-X Tokyo Purple #6 — $1.50
- ☐ 40-494-8 Baja Bandidos #7 — $1.50
- ☐ 40-495-6 Northwest Contract #8 — $1.50
- ☐ 40-425-5 Dodge City Bombers #9 — $1.50
- ☐ 40-957-5 Bloody Boston #12 — $1.50
- ☐ 40-426-3 Dixie Death Squad #13 — $1.50
- ☐ 40-427-1 Mankill Sport #14 — $1.50
- ☐ 40-851-X Quebec Connection #15 — $1.50
- ☐ 40-851-X Deepsea Shootout #16 — $1.50
- ☐ 40-428-X Countdown to Terror #18 — $1.50
- ☐ 40-258-9 Radiation Hit #20 — $1.50
- ☐ 40-079-9 Supergun Mission #21 — $1.25
- ☐ 40-067-5 High Disaster #22 — $1.50
- ☐ 40-085-3 Divine Death #23 — $1.50
- ☐ 40-177-9 Cryogenic Nightmare #24 — $1.50
- ☐ 40-178-7 Floating Death #25 — $1.50
- ☐ 40-179-5 Mexican Brown #26 — $1.50
- ☐ 40-268-6 Skyhigh Betrayers #28 — $1.50
- ☐ 40-269-4 Aryan Onslaught #29 — $1.50
- ☐ 40-270-8 Computer Kill #30 — $1.50
- ☐ 40-363-1 Oklahoma Firefight #31 — $1.50
- ☐ 40-514-6 Showbiz Wipeout #32 — $1.50
- ☐ 40-513-8 Satellite Slaughter #33 — $1.50
- ☐ 40-631-2 Death Ray Terror #34 — $1.50
- ☐ 40-632-0 Black Massacre #35 — $1.75
- ☐ 40-674-6 Candidate's Blood #37 — $1.75
- ☐ 40-924-9 Cruise Into Chaos #39 — $1.75
- ☐ 41-114-6 Assassination Factor #40 — $1.75
- ☐ 41-116-2 Hell's Hostages #41 — $1.75
- ☐ 41-157-X Rampage in Rio #43 — $1.95

Buy them at your local bookstore or use this handy coupon

Clip and mail this page with your order

PINNACLE BOOKS, INC.—Reader Service Dept.
1430 Broadway, New York, NY 10018

Please send me the book(s) I have checked above. I am enclosing $_____ (please add 75¢ to cover postage and handling). Send check or money order only—no cash or C.O.D.'s.

Mr./Mrs./Miss _____

Address _____

City _____ State/Zip _____

Please allow six weeks for delivery. Prices subject to change without notice.

NEW FROM AMERICA'S #1 SERIES PUBLISHER!
MARK MANDELL

NAZI HUNTER

Born from the smoldering embers of the Nazi holocaust, American career soldier Curt Jaeger, the son of a Nazi war criminal responsible for the murder of millions, vows vengeance against his own father...and all living relics of the Third Reich around the world. Swift and savage, he will spare his quarry no rest...no peace... until he has scattered their bones in the wind.

☐ 41-049-2 NAZI HUNTER $2.50

Buy them at your local bookstore or use this handy coupon
Clip and mail this page with your order

 PINNACLE BOOKS, INC.—Reader Service Dept.
1430 Broadway, New York, NY 10018

Please send me the book(s) I have checked above. I am enclosing $_____ (please add 75¢ to cover postage and handling). Send check or money order only—no cash or C.O.D.'s.

Mr./Mrs./Miss _____

Address _____

City _____ State/Zip _____

Please allow six weeks for delivery. Prices subject to change without notice.

More bestselling western adventure from Pinnacle, America's #1 series publisher. Over 6 million copies of EDGE in print!

☐ 41-279-7 Loner #1	$1.75	☐ 40-585-5 Rhapsody in Red #21	$1.50
☐ 41-280-0 Ten Grand #2	$1.75	☐ 40-487-5 Slaughter Road #22	$1.50
☐ 41-769-1 Apache Death #3	$1.95	☐ 40-485-9 Echoes of War #23	$1.50
☐ 41-282-7 Killer's Breed #4	$1.75	☐ 41-302-5 Slaughterday #24	$1.75
☐ 40-507-3 Blood on Silver #5	$1.50	☐ 41-303-3 Violence Trail #25	$1.75
☐ 41-770-5 Red River #6	$1.95	☐ 40-579-0 Savage Dawn #26	$1.50
☐ 41-285-1 California Kill #7	$1.75	☐ 41-309-2 Death Drive #27	$1.75
☐ 41-286-X Hell's Seven #8	$1.75	☐ 40-204-X Eve of Evil #28	$1.50
☐ 41-287-8 Bloody Summer #9	$1.75	☐ 41-775-6 The Living, The Dying, and The Dead #29	$1.95
☐ 41-771-3 Black Vengeance #10	$1.95	☐ 41-312-2 Towering Nightmare #30	$1.75
☐ 41-289-4 Sioux Uprising #11	$1.75	☐ 41-313-0 Guilty Ones #31	$1.75
☐ 41-290-8 Death's Bounty #12	$1.75	☐ 41-314-9 Frightened Gun #32	$1.75
☐ 40-462-X Hated #13	$1.50	☐ 41-315-7 Red Fury #33	$1.75
☐ 41-772-1 Tiger's Gold #14	$1.95	☐ 40-865-X A Ride in the Sun #34	$1.75
☐ 41-293-2 Paradise Loses #15	$1.75	☐ 41-776-4 Death Deal #35	$1.95
☐ 41-294-0 Final Shot #16	$1.75	☐ 40-867-6 Town on Trial #36	$1.75
☐ 40-584-7 Vengeance Valley #17	$1.50	☐ 41-448-X Vengeance at Ventura #37	$1.75
☐ 41-773-X Ten Tombstones #18	$1.95	☐ 41-106-5 Two of a Kind	$1.75
☐ 41-297-5 Ashes and Dust #19	$1.75		
☐ 41-774-8 Sullivan's Law #20	$1.95		

Canadian orders must be paid with U.S. Bank check or U.S. Postal money order only.

Buy them at your local bookstore or use this handy coupon
Clip and mail this page with your order

PINNACLE BOOKS, INC.—Reader Service Dept.
1430 Broadway, New York, N.Y. 10018

Please send me the book(s) I have checked above. I am enclosing $_____
(please add 75¢ to cover postage and handling). Send check or money order only—no cash or C.O.D.'s.

Mr./Mrs./Miss_____

Address_____

City_____ State/Zip_____

Please allow six weeks for delivery. Prices subject to change without notice.

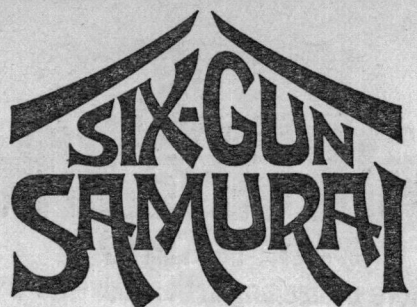

SIX-GUN SAMURAI

by Patrick Lee

FROM THE LAND OF THE SHOGUNS AND AMERICA'S #1 SERIES PUBLISHER, AN EXCITING NEW ACTION/ADVENTURE SERIES THAT COMBINES FAR-EASTERN TRADITION WITH HARDCORE WESTERN VIOLENCE!

Stranded in Japan, American-born Tom Fletcher becomes immersed in the ancient art of bushido—a violent code demanding bravery, honor and ultimate sacrifice—and returns to his homeland on a bloodsoaked trail of vengeance.

☐ 41-190-1	SIX-GUN SAMURAI #1	$1.95
☐ 41-191-X	SIX-GUN SAMURAI #2 Bushido Vengeance	$1.95
☐ 41-192-8	SIX-GUN SAMURAI #3 Gundown at Golden Gate	$1.95
☐ 41-416-1	SIX-GUN SAMURAI #4 Kamikaze Justice	$1.95

Buy them at your local bookstore or use this handy coupon
Clip and mail this page with your order

PINNACLE BOOKS, INC.—Reader Service Dept.
1430 Broadway, New York, NY 10018

Please send me the book(s) I have checked above. I am enclosing $_____ (please add 75¢ to cover postage and handling). Send check or money order only—no cash or C.O.D.'s.

Mr./Mrs./Miss _____

Address _____

City _____ State/Zip _____

Please allow six weeks for delivery. Prices subject to change without notice.
Canadian orders must be paid with U.S. Bank check or U.S. Postal money order only.

DEATH MERCHANT
by Joseph Rosenberger

More bestselling action/adventure from Pinnacle, America's #1 series publisher— Over 6 million copies in print!

☐ 41-345-9 Death Merchant #1	$1.95		☐ 40-117-5 Enigma Project #25	$1.25
☐ 41-346-7 Operation Overkill #2	$1.95		☐ 40-118-3 Mexican Hit #26	$1.50
☐ 41-347-5 Psychotron Plot #3	$1.95		☐ 40-119-1 Surinam Affair #27	$1.50
☐ 41-348-3 Chinese Conspiracy #4	$1.95		☐ 40-833-1 Nipponese Nightmare #28	$1.75
☐ 41-349-1 Satan Strike #5	$1.95		☐ 40-272-1 Fatal Formula #29	$1.50
☐ 41-350-5 Albanian Connection #6	$1.95		☐ 40-385-2 Shambhala Strike #30	$1.50
☐ 41-351-3 Castro File #7	$1.95		☐ 40-392-5 Operation Thunderbolt #31	$1.50
☐ 41-352-1 Billionaire Mission #8	$1.95		☐ 40-475-1 Deadly Manhunt #32	$1.50
☐ 41-353-X Laser War #9	$1.95		☐ 40-476-X Alaska Conspiracy #33	*$1.50
☐ 41-354-8 Mainline Plot #10	$1.95		☐ 41-378-5 Operation Mind-Murder #34	$1.95
☐ 40-816-1 Manhattan Wipeout #11	$1.75		☐ 40-478-6 Massacre in Rome #35	$1.50
☐ 40-817-X KGB Frame #12	$1.75		☐ 41-380-7 Cosmic Reality Kill #36	$1.95
☐ 40-497-2 Mato Grosso Horror #13	$1.50		☐ 41-382-3 The Burning Blue Death #38	$1.95
☐ 40-819-6 Vengeance: Golden Hawk #14	$1.75		☐ 41-383-1 The Fourth Reich #39	$1.95
☐ 22-823-6 Iron Swastika Plot #15	$1.25		☐ 41-020-4 High Command Murder #42	$1.95
☐ 22-857-0 Invasion of the Clones #16	$1.25		☐ 41-021-2 Devil's Trashcan #43	$1.95
☐ 22-880-5 Zemlya Expedition #17	$1.25		☐ 41-326-2 The Rim of Fire Conspiracy #45	$1.95
☐ 22-911-9 Nightmare in Algeria #18	$1.25		☐ 41-327-0 Blood Bath #46	$1.95
☐ 40-460-3 Armageddon, USA! #19	$1.50		☐ 41-328-9 Operation Skyhook #47	$1.95
☐ 40-256-2 Hell in Hindu Land #20	$1.50		☐ 41-644-X The Psionics War #48	$1.95
☐ 40-826-9 Pole Star Secret #21	$1.75			
☐ 40-827-7 Kondrashev Chase #22	$1.75			
☐ 40-078-0 Budapest Action #23	$1.25			
☐ 40-352-6 Kronos Plot #24	$1.50			

Buy them at your local bookstore or use this handy coupon
Clip and mail this page with your order

PINNACLE BOOKS, INC.—Reader Service Dept.
1430 Broadway, New York, NY 10018

Please send me the book(s) I have checked above. I am enclosing $_____ (please add 75¢ to cover postage and handling). Send check or money order only—no cash or C.O.D.'s.

Mr./Mrs./Miss _____

Address _____

City _____ State/Zip _____

Please allow six weeks for delivery. Prices subject to change without notice.